Nothing is hotter than a summer day in New Orleans, Louisiana without air conditioning and only two blades on your ceiling fan. Everything in life seemed normal until my first vivid memory of my early childhood. My mom and dad never lived together past my infancy so I was thrilled to spend the evening with him after my first day of first grade. I sat in my room at my mother's house in the seventh ward of New Orleans drenched in sweat as I waited for my father to arrive. My dad was a very active father. There weren't many of those in the neighborhood I grew up in. An active father was an anomaly in my hood. There was an explosion of violence in the 1990's and the city became known throughout the country as the murder capital. Children, women, and other innocent civilians were not spared from the crimes that occurred during the historic crime wave in New Orleans. Regardless of the consistent reckless crimes that took place in my neighborhood I could not wait to get out of the house. My house made a sauna feel like a deep freezer and I could not wait to show my father off when we walked the streets. My father promised me he would walk with me to the corner store to get a po-boy as soon as he arrived. After thirty minutes of sweating up a storm in my bedroom I heard my dad's diesel truck pull up outside over the constant noise in my neighborhood. We started walking to the corner store to get some po-boys immediately after my father arrived. Before we could make it around the corner a fight broke out between two teenagers across the street from my house. The fight turned one sided fairly quick. The guy who swung the first punch lost his footing then was dropped to the ground by two powerful punches to the face. Fighting was a normalcy in my hood. It was similar to jail in the aspect that if you won the fight your reputation would climb, and if you lost, you knew more people would start trying you. It was also similar to jail in the sense of regularity. I

1

stopped in my tracks to watch the fight. Then my dad pushed me in the direction of the corner store and yelled at me, "Don't you ever stop to watch a fight in the hood. They rarely end with two people going their separate ways in peace." My dad spent the rest of the walk to the corner store lecturing me on what else not to do in the hood.

When my dad and I finally made it to the corner store we parted ways because the po-boys were on the opposite side of the store from where I spotted my two friends, Pickle and Skip. Both of my friends were acting extremely weird when I greeted them. Pickle acted very standoffish which was unusual. He wanted to hang around the front of the store. Skip lured me to the back of the store because he said we needed to talk. Once we got to the back of the store Skip pushed me. I was befuddled as of why because we never got into any altercations before and he pushed me with minimal force. I stepped to Skip and asked, "Why did you push me?" He whispered, "Just push me back." Lick for lick was a common game we played in New Orleans so I figured he wanted to play push for push. I pushed Skip back with the same force he pushed me with. After I pushed him he flopped and knocked over three stands of snacks causing an unnecessary scene. There were only two employees present at the store. The owner who was working at the front register and the cook who was working at the back of the store. The owner left the register unattended to tend to the situation that Skip caused by knocking over the merchandise. As soon as the owner was about twenty feet away from the register Pickle hopped over the counter and emptied the cash out of the register. By the time the owner noticed what was going on Pickle and Skip had already vacated the premises. I was unknowingly used as an accessory to theft. The owner knew I had no involvement because I entered the store with my father, and Skip and Pickle were well known troublemakers throughout the neighborhood. My dad laid into me again on the way back home from the corner store. I kept my head down for majority of the walk back to my house. For some reason I lifted my

2

head back up when we made it to the end of the block by my house and my life would never be the same again.

The guy who got beat up across the street from my house was chasing after the person who beat him up. I wondered why would the person who just won the fight was running from the person who he just beat up. While they ran I saw nothing else but them two. All of my other surroundings such as the public housing development, and the bar room across the street were a blur to me. After giving chase for an entire city block, the guy who got beat up stopped running and reached into his waist. He whipped out the first gun I ever saw in my life and let off three shots in the guy's back who beat him up. The guy who won the fight laid lifeless directly across the street from my house in a pool of blood. I instantly looked back and the killer was out of sight. The killer vanished before I could set eyes on him again. Not seeing the killer provoked me to wonder how long I was in another world for during that occurrence. That killing put me in another world for the rest of my life. I was the tender age of five when I witnessed my first murder. I was constantly reminded of it every day in my childhood and adolescence because it happened across the street from the house where I would spend the first fifteen years of my life residing. My childhood was snatched from me like the victim's life who I watched get slain at five years old. It ran off with the killer who laid a man flat in broad daylight. I could no longer be an innocent child after learning that the next moment in life is not guaranteed because I witnessed a cold blooded murder. As a child I experienced something most adults had not witnessed. Witnessing a homicide as a child made me grow up quick and gave me an enhanced appreciation for life. One would be inclined to assume that witnessing a murder in the first grade would be the toughest memory of my life. Would you believe me if I told you witnessing a murder in first grade was not even one of my top five worst memories in life?

Chapter 2

A memory that was definitely in my top five worst memories was getting put off of the college basketball team that I had always dreamed of playing on. My dad introduced me to basketball three weeks after I witnessed my first homicide. My elementary school almost held me back in the first grade because I missed three weeks of school in a row from being so shook up from the first murder I witnessed. My dad broke me out of my funk by taking me to play basketball in a gym for the first time. The thoughts of the murder never existed when I was on the basketball court. Being taken away from the pain in life when I played basketball was what made me fall in love with the game. Now that basketball was gone, I only had one other coping mechanism. Smoking weed was a coping mechanism superior to any prescription pill that any doctor could have given me for "Post Traumatic Stress Disorder". The use of it was the reason I got put off the collegiate basketball team. I was fortunate to have a teammate in college who I played basketball with since I was an adolescent. Pain is intensified when you have no one to go through it with and if no one was there to watch it happen. Brandon had far more sympathy for me than most of my family. He was there for my years of sweat, blood, and tears I gave to basketball and also watched it go to waste over a half of blunt. He texted me an hour after I got put off the team and told me he would bring me some weed later that night.

Brandon dropped the weed off but did not want to smoke because of what just happened to me. One of the many great things about New Orleans is that there are an abundance of double houses and one of my best friends Hassan lived next door in the double we shared. Hassan caught me walking from Brandon's truck and asked me, "Where is the weed at? I already heard what happened with the basketball team. I'm going to buy some for us, and my cousin wants some to." Brandon gave me a bag of weed that was worth $30 for free and I sold it to Hassan for $40. After me and Hassan finished smoking, his cousin called him back and asked for a $100 bag of the same kind he had just purchased. When I pulled out my phone to call Brandon, I had a message that had been waiting unread in my inbox for two hours. "Hey, the dorms got raided so I left an ounce for you on the side of your porch." Hassan and I sold half of the bag that night and that was the birth of my career as an illegal entrepreneur.

When most athletes career end an overwhelming percentage search for opportunities that could scratch their competitive itch. I had no clue what would scratch mine. I thought my itch would be scratched by a non-paid internship I was awarded during my sophomore year in college, but it wasn't. There was nothing competitive about the internship. My responsibilities were to obtain intake information from the newly arrested inmates at Orleans Parish Prison and to sit through bond hearings. I searched for a job from my freshman year of college until the end of my basketball career and was unsuccessful at landing one despite the fact that I attended a top fifty university in the country. Finding a job wasn't even about scratching a competitive itch anymore. I needed food in my stomach and money to pay for school. Dropping out of college was not an option. I became desperate to find a job. I even applied to become a garbage man and they didn't hire me. It was time to implement the only thing I learned from my internship at the jailhouse, how not to get caught. I figured with my street smarts and my knowledge on how not to get caught that I could generate enough money by hustling to pay my tuition and avoid getting put out of college.

When I woke up the next morning it felt like it was the first day of school and the prior night was my orientation. I had no obligations during the morning time, and that wasn't the case for the past three years. Although I did not set my alarm clock, I woke up at the same time I did every morning. Surprisingly, I could not go back to sleep. I sat in the bed and let everything set in for an hour. Before I could get to the sink to brush my teeth, I heard a few knocks on the door and a few rings from the doorbell. It had to be the witnesses of Jehovah, but it was too early for them to come knocking. It was Hassan on the other side of the peephole. It was the same time that we met on the porch every morning to smoke before I started playing basketball in college. Before I could open the door all of the way Hassan got straight to the point and asked, "Do you have more of the same weed from last night? I have someone who wants to cop some." By lunch time we moved the rest of the ounce. Majority of the customers came from Hassan, so I asked him did he want some money. Hassan had a better idea, he just wanted me to give him something to smoke. That was the first time I experienced bartering.

Thankfully Brandon was available to bring me another ounce after his morning practice, but one ounce was not enough to satisfy my growing demand from customers. When Brandon brought over the second ounce he made the most unique transaction I had up until then. Usually a drug dealer wants a quick and smooth transaction to escape a potentially violent situation. He wanted to have a conversation before we made the transaction. He told me the coaching staff was disappointed that I did not show up the next morning after getting put off of the team to try to get back on. I didn't give a rebuttal because I was scared of the truth. I had found a new passion in hustling and lost my passion for basketball. I honestly did not want to play anymore. I told him I would call the coaches later that evening to change the conversation. After I saw that Brandon only had an ounce he could sell me I was prompted to ask him a big question. I hesitantly looked at him and said, "I need to meet your connect." Drug dealers are usually super reluctant to let a customer meet their connect. I was astonished that he responded, "Sure, I will introduce you to him tomorrow morning when I re-up. I will pick you up at 10:00am tomorrow morning."

Brandon caught me off guard by arriving at 9:45am the next morning. Early for him was stumbling in five minutes late. As soon as I got in the car, I noticed white residue and coffee in the cup holder. I knew this was about to be a life changing morning. Before he could ask me what's up, he began giving me the rundown on the plug. "Derrick is his name. He is from Harlem, New York, 6 foot 5, 300 pounds, and is one of the best dressers and talkers that ever graced this earth." I was intrigued by his energy and openness. It was obvious he was experiencing a caffeine and cocaine high at the same time. "Tell me more", I said. Brandon responded, "The biggest thing is when Derrick looks at you in the eyes he stares through your soul, but has the biggest sense of humor so he can easily catch you off guard. You never know if he is joking or dead serious so stay on your toes. He is also accompanied by a minimum of four people on each move he makes." He had told me all I needed to know about Derrick, so my mind zoned out imagining how this interaction would go.

It was a forty minute drive so I must have been in la-la land for a significant amount of time because a gun tapping on the driver's window woke me up from my daydream. Ever since I was five years old I had paranoia and anxiety about being around guns. "Get out of the car", is what I heard simultaneously with the gun tapping on the window. Brandon scurried to attention like he was in the military. He never exhibited that same hustle on the basketball court, so it took everything in me not to laugh at him. The humungous guy tapping the gun on the window had to be Derrick. He had on a bullet grey Gucci track jacket and every other article of clothing he had on appeared to be just as exclusive. As I checked out the rest of his fit, he approached me. I shook his hand and gave him a compliment. "I like this cat. My name is Spike", he said. I took no offense to him lying, and not wanting to tell me his government name. The fake name may have been him protecting his identity until he could trust me or just a display of his sense of humor. Spike went back to the front of his lime green truck and tapped on the hood with his gun and said, "Come here fellas. I want y'all to meet somebody." Four guys who looked like they were responsible for forty bodies each hopped out of the truck and embraced me with all of the manners in the world. The guy who got out of the passenger seat gave Spike a duffle bag. Spike looked at Brandon, then looked at me, then did the same thing three times in a row and said, "Boy, you lucky I like who you running with. Here you hold one ounce." Then he walked up to me and said, "Here, I'm going to let you hold two ounces." I need you to be my New Orleans protégé. Y'all report back to me by sunrise Monday, and if y'all don't. Y'all won't be alive to see the sunset Monday." As we got back in the car, my thirst for opportunity drowned any other possible negative thoughts or feelings that could have come to mind. All I could do was think about money. I couldn't say the same thing for Brandon. His cocaine and caffeine high had finally worn off, and all he did was talk about worse case scenarios. It was only 11:00am, but let his face tell it, it was 11:00pm. Before I knew it we were back at my house. After Brandon parked he said, "Thanks for listening bro." Little did he know I didn't hear shit he said on the entire ride home?

I spent the rest of that day hustling by myself. My training wheels were off. I served five people by the pay phone a block up from my house, and made several hundred dollars. I was out of customers that I could serve by myself and Hassan was still at work so I decided to hit up my favorite po-boy restaurant which was a few streets away from my house. While I was waiting in line surveying the menu I felt someone looking at me in my peripheral vision. Next I heard a sweet little laugh directed towards me. Wow, it was Bianca from high school. I was even more surprised that she was acknowledging me, being that she barely even interacted with anyone we went to high school with. Bianca had grown up quick. She started clubbing as a sophomore in high school, and only dated grown men during her high school years. She also only hung with grown women, so essentially she didn't deal with anyone at our school. I wanted to hug her, but all I could do was stare at her whisky colored skin, full lips, and tablespoon shaped butt. Before I could ask her how she was doing, she asked, "What are you ordering? The whole left side of the menu with your high ass?" I didn't know if the joke was that funny because I was obviously high or if I was just so happy that she was joking with me, but I laughed until tears came out of my eyes. As I surveyed the premises while laughing, I noticed she wasn't with anyone. "Who are you with?" I asked. She replied, "I am with you."

Normally if someone you liked for years gave you attention you would get nervous. I didn't feel an ounce of nervousness. We sat in the corner of the restaurant isolated by ourselves for an hour. That hour felt like an eternity. After we finished our food, I asked her the bravest question ever. I asked her if she wanted to follow me to my house. She said, "I can do you one better. I'll leave my car here and hop in with you." My father always told me to be ready when success comes, but I never fully understood what it meant until that night. I had condoms, a clean crib, and a lot of energy. The timing could not have been any more perfect. As soon as she got in my car she turned my radio off and said, "She only wanted to hear me, and that I had her undivided attention." The feeling of having a person sexually who you deemed untouchable is pure ecstasy. Before I knew it, we were having sex for two hours. The only reason that made me realize how much time went by was because of the doorbell. If you have an unexpected visitor at your door at midnight, you know it's time to get your gun. My dad who I shared the house with but was rarely there had an arsenal of guns at the house. However they were all upstairs and that wasn't convenient for time's sake. It could have been the beginning of a home invasion. Bianca got up and ran to her purse which was under my computer table and pulled out two guns. "Which one do you want?" she said in a super laid back voice as if she were asking me do I want drums or flats. Five people were killed on my street in the past month, so the sense of urgency erased me noticing that it wasn't normal for a woman to have two guns in her purse. I chose the biggest gun and crept to the door like I was a secret agent. I resided in a shotgun house, so the walk to the door made me feel like I was in a video game and it gave me a sense of anticipation to greet the situation at the front door. As I got to the door I felt a wet hand on my lower back. The wet hand on my lower back caused me to make a noise that could be heard through the front door and probably across the street. The unwarranted noise, plus having an exclusive female on my back gave me no choice but to drop my nuts and swing open the door like I heard opportunity knocking.

It was Hassan behind the door. I slammed the door in his face. Hassan went to high school with me and Bianca. My forefathers always preached to me to keep a woman's actions in the bedroom, in the bedroom. I told her who it was at the door and she ran back into the room. As I watched her beautiful brown ass bounce back to my room I almost forgot my boy was at the door until he rang the doorbell three more times. Hassan had the biggest smile on his face waiting for me behind the door. I wondered why he was on my porch smiling at midnight. Hassan said, "Man you won't believe who I saw at the po-boy spot." I was expecting him to say maybe a professional athlete or entertainer due to his excitement and the popular crowd that the po-boy spot had been attracting lately. I asked, "Was it an actress?" He said, "No, even better. I saw Bianca at the po-boy spot." That statement is indicative of how highly she was thought of. I don't know where this defensiveness came from, but I sharply responded, "How do you know for sure that was her?" "Come on man, who else has a brand new candy apple red colored sports car in the hood?", Hassan responded. "Did you talk to her?" I asked. He said "Oh no. I didn't say anything. You know how stuck up she be acting." Normally I would agree, but I just had her stuck up against my bedroom wall, so I just said, "I guess, but what's up?" In a rushed voice Hassan said, "Sell me an ounce, I got some more people that want some." I went back to my bedroom to bag up what he needed. Bianca intercepted me in the kitchen which was on my way to my bedroom, and handed me my scale and weed. I weighed up what Hassan wanted and made the quickest hand to hand transaction known to mankind. As I got back to the kitchen she led me by the hand to the bedroom. Any person knows there is no better feeling than being consensually led by hand to the bedroom. When we got back to my room we had more bone chilling sex until almost daybreak.

I was fortunate enough to wake up before her the next morning so I could recap the eventful night in peace. When I opened my eyes and turned over, I couldn't do anything but glance at the woman who was built like a statue as she lay in my bed with a smile on her face while she was asleep. I wondered what she was dreaming about, but it was too much of a new situation for me to sit there and stare. The first thing I did every morning was brush my teeth. To my surprise, a perfectly rolled blunt was left for me by my toothbrush. I couldn't do anything but sit on the edge of the tub and look up at the skies to thank the man above for my previous night. My doorbell rang and I already knew it was Hassan. As soon as I crossed the threshold Hassan hugged me as if we won the super bowl. I didn't know if what he purchased from me was that great or something else happened. He couldn't hold back and said, "I saw Bianca coming out of your house to grab something from in your truck after I left last night." Hassan was someone who stalked the streets when the sun went down so he knew everything that went on in the hood before it finished happening. I couldn't even lie like I wanted to and say that we did not spend the night together last night. Our cover was blown and I had no choice but to tell my brother that she stayed the night, and I left the rest for his imagination then I smoothly changed the conversation. Even though we switched topics Hassan still gave me the look a proud father would give his son for the duration of our conversation. My phone rang consistently throughout our entire conversation. Usually I would give whoever I was with at the time my undivided attention, but after the ninth time my phone rang I had to check it. I had eight inquiries and one text to come back inside to have morning sex. I had to cut my conversation short with Hassan, duty called. Time was of the essence to

11

make these transactions happen. Besides the eight calls I missed, my girl said she needed three more ounces to sell as if I had them in the pantry next to the minute rice. I had no choice but to figure out a way to get in touch with Spike. To kill time I asked my girl did she want me to bring her to the po-boy spot to get her car. When I left the house that chilly morning, it was very reminiscent of August 29, 2005, when Hurricane Katrina happened. I knew life would never be the same again.

Chapter 3

It was amazing that my girl's brand new red sports car was untampered with when we pulled up back at the po-boy spot. Bianca insisted on sitting down and eating po-boys together before we got on with the rest of the day. She eased my mind with her calmness and surety that everything would workout. After we walked out of the restaurant a yellow sports utility vehicle came flying down the street. Whenever you see a car flying down the street in the hood, no matter who you are you have to consider that it might be a drive by. But I had to play tough and act like I didn't see it. Plus, what were the odds someone would be dumb enough to do a drive by in a yellow SUV during broad daylight? To my surprise, the SUV swerved to the curb and slammed on its brakes directly in front of us. It took everything in me to act like I was ready for whatever was waiting behind the driver's side window. It was a stare down between me and the driver's side limo tinted windows. The window finally rolled down, and it was Spike sitting behind it. I told my girl to wait for me in her car. He told me to jump in. When I got in the SUV Spike said, "Damn black, I love how you moving in these streets. Did she buy her own po-boy?" I responded, "Yes, and mines" He laughed for a second then wiped the smile off his face and asked, "How are you moving with the work I gave you?" I reached into my pocket and counted the money I had made from him fronting me plus more. After I finished counting the money he told me, "Get the fuck out of the car." Pulling money out of my pocket and being braggadocios was not my style. I wondered if I just caused things to go left. I guess they went right, because he gave me a hug and yelled, "That's what the fuck I'm talking about. One day you are going to graduate from a foot soldier and this city will be yours." I felt as if my whole life dreams had just changed. Spike went in his trunk and gave me double of what he gave me last time, and said, "Don't tell Brandon I gave you this either." Then he pulled off.

As soon as I got in my girl's car she said, "I don't like him." "How could you not like a man that has me eating on these streets?" I asked her with a baffled look on my face. She responded, "He is going to have you in jail eating to. After we move this I'm going to introduce you to somebody who won't get you indicted." I thought to myself, how many new people am I going to get involved in my life this weekend. It felt like the sun went down so fast. Before I knew it we sold everything Spike had fronted me. It was only twenty-four hours I spent with her, but I couldn't help but think about spending the rest of my life with her. She was an aid to my dream. I started doing the math on how life would be if she was by my side every day. I asked her on a date later that night and she said, "No I am going to take you on one." To my surprise she already had a bag of clothes in her trunk so we went to my house to get dressed and headed to one of the most popular steakhouses in New Orleans.

It was a packed restaurant and so was the waiting area. After thirty seconds of waiting a hostess asked us to follow her. I asked my girl had she made reservations, and she responded, "You love to interview people don't you?" I let that question be rhetorical. As we walked toward the back of the restaurant I felt everyone looking at us as we walked past them. It was similar to when you are high and you think everyone in the world is watching you, however I wasn't high and everyone was actually watching us. The hostess led us to a door that looked like a janitor closet was behind it. When she opened the door it looked like the setting of the last supper. The only person in the room was sitting at the head of the table. He was a short African man who had on some beige pants that were the same length as yoga pants, a pink Burberry dress shirt, and a small gold chain that looked extremely expensive. His name was Uriah. I automatically knew he was a person who would change my life. I didn't know in which way, but a black man who looked like a fortune even when he was trying to hide it became an automatic inspiration to me. Growing up in the neighborhood drug dealers are the master misconceptions. They had fancy clothes, beautiful women, shiny jewelry, and fancy cars. None of which added to their net worth. I knew from the jump Uriah was different.

When I sat down at the table it was a feeling I never felt before. It was similar to when I sat down to interview at a hotel downtown which was a dream job to me, but the twist was I had the girl of my dreams sitting in with me this time. A panel interview didn't have shit on this. The first question he asked me was a universal trick question. He asked, "What did I want to be when I grow up?" Someone is mentally sizing you up when they ask you that. If you have a prestigious answer such as a doctor, lawyer, or an engineer the person who asked that question is automatically impressed. If you are still in limbo a person responds with discomfort, which is a disrespectful thing to do, although most people do it in an unconscious manner. I always had rebuttals no matter what I was asked, but I was caught off guard by his question. I looked at my girl after he asked me that question then he asked me, "Do you want to be like her when you grow up?" The ice was beyond broke when he asked me that. I responded, "I want to be like you when I grow up, alive and wealthy." He said, "That was a great answer. You have no choice but to be like me if you are going to be dating a queen like my niece. It took a lot of balls

14

to humble yourself in front of such a beautiful woman. If you are dating my niece you have to be a compliment to her. She has been moving product for me since you all were in grade school, and now it's time for her to fall back from the game. With that being said you have a perfect opportunity to walk into our family business." I felt the most sensitive touch on my back and it was the waitress. She said, "Welcome into the restaurant and into the family. I am Patty and I am here to serve you." It was beyond my belief that when I turned to my girl she smiled and did not say anything about the waitress touching me in that manner. The waitress said, "I know what you want and it will be out in ten minutes. I know you will be pleased." When my food came out it was exactly what I wanted. A porterhouse steak with lobster macaroni and cheese. It felt like everyone around me knew what I wanted in life. Brandon knew I needed weed in my life, Derrick knew I needed to be fronted, my girl knew exactly what type of girl I needed, and she knew I needed a new plug. As I sat across from my new connect, Uriah, I still didn't know exactly what I wanted in life. I was tripping with no map. After halfway through my dinner I knew that bullshitting my way through the conversation approach would not work with him. He asked the question after the question, he read your body language, and felt your energy. At least I bullshitted my way to the part of the conversation that I needed to set myself up for the win. Uriah said he is open to fronting me, but then asked what would he be getting out of this. Loyalty is one of the most important traits to have in the streets, so I went with that for a response.

When it was time to leave the restaurant Uriah gave me a firm handshake and stared through my soul then said, "Leave your car where it is. My head dealer has to ride a certain way, plus my niece doesn't like manual windows." When me and my girl got in the car she put her head in my lap and didn't lift her head up until we got back to my house. After I put the vehicle in park Bianca lifted her head up and was surprised to see we were back at my house. My girl displayed an attitude that I heard she possessed but I never personally experienced before. She cut her eyes at me and said, "I hope you don't think we are staying in for the night. We have money to make. This is morning time for you. Let's go weigh this up and hit the streets." By the time the sun came up we had made a few thousand dollars. We got in the house around 6:00am. The same time a normal party ends in New Orleans. Me and my girl slept the morning and afternoon away. I usually don't dream, but I had a dream about Brandon. In the dream I was yelling his name as he was sinking in quicksand. As soon as I woke up I called him before I could wipe the cold out of my eyes. When Brandon answered the phone he yelled, "I am not going to make it to see Tuesday morning, I have only sold one fourth of what Derrick fronted me", before I could even say hello. My dream made a lot of sense. I don't think he would have made it to see Tuesday's sunrise if I didn't have that dream because I would have for sure forgotten to call him and I knew he would not have called me. My weekend was so hectic that I forgot I was in business with him. I asked my girl could we meet up later after I handled this situation with Brandon. As she was leaving she said, "It is time for you to get a team. I have shown you enough to where you can have people working for you. Figure that out soon because my uncle is expecting you to put some more people on so y'all can move more weight.

I thought about how easygoing Spike was and he already had an intolerance for the way Brandon moved. Therefore, I knew he would not be a good fit to work for me if I was going to handle work from Spike and Uriah. He could not even handle what Spike was fronting to him. I was clueless on which direction to go. I had time to figure out who I wanted to work for me so the priority was to help him live to see the sunrise Tuesday morning. It took me thirty minutes to sell the rest of Brandon's product. We were prepared to meet with Spike the next morning. I wondered if I would have to decide about making a decision to just get fronted by one person or two people. The last thing you wanted to be is late with a drug dealer's money. I didn't know which direction I would go if I had to choose one. Spike and Brandon introduced me to the game, but Bianca and Uriah introduced me to a new level. Brandon and Bianca had been in the game way before me, but my girl gave me more game in two days than what he could have given me in two years.

When I met with Spike I gave him more money than what he expected, therefore he returned the favor and gave me more product than what I expected. He actually gave me the same amount that Uriah did. Brandon got the same skimpy package as he got last time. My decision to continue doing business with both of them was made because I still had nowhere close to the money I needed to pay my upcoming tuition payment and I still didn't get a job offer. From that transaction I learned the concept of under promising and over delivering. It was something to live by going forward. The ride back from Spike was another quiet one for me. All I could do was game plan. I was close to Brandon, but I was not ready to open up with him about Uriah because he was of no relevance to the situation.

Three weeks had went by and I had no idea who to put on. There was no YouTube or Google to help me figure that out. I continued to meet up with Uriah and Spike on a weekly basis. Uriah continued to let me drive his big body foreign car on everyday besides Thursday. Thursday had arrived and it was the first day that I had an almost empty schedule since I started hustling, so it was a perfect day to figure out who would be hustling on my team. I had no choice but to reach out for help. My best friend Lamont and I didn't talk on an everyday basis, and looking at our text messages it had been three months since we last spoke. Any great friendship can pick up where it left off. I called him for advice on building a team and we talked the whole entire morning like we didn't miss a day talking to each other. Lamont was in north Louisiana hustling to pay for his college tuition also. He had a situation opposite of mines. He had an extremely strong team and no good connections. I had great connects and a team that was nonexistent. Lamont gave me advice that I could not believe I didn't think of. Involve Hassan full time. The whole entire city knew and respected Hassan. He used to hustle before Hurricane Katrina but stopped because his plug died during the storm. I called Hassan and asked if he wanted a steak dinner.

Hassan was born in Liberia, Africa and moved to the United States at twelve years old after his parents were killed in the First Liberian Civil War. He moved to the U.S with his sister who was fifteen years old at the time. After two years of being in New Orleans, his sister was killed during a home invasion and Hassan took care of himself ever since then. He sold drugs before he could fluently speak English. I was a fool not to think to involve him full time. When Hassan got in the car I got straight to the point as soon as he sat down. On the way to the steak house Hassan was very reluctant to start back hustling. He had been through almost everything in the game but death. Hassan had been jailed, robbed, shot up, you name it. He gave me pushback, but I knew I had two things working in my favor. Hassan stayed next door to me so, I knew he wanted out of the hood just as bad as I did. Also, he was like a brother to me and he knew I needed him on this venture to help pay for college. When we got to the steakhouse they directed us to the back where Uriah usually hosted me.

While the USA is one of the wealthiest countries in the nation, it has one of the highest income inequalities in the world. Growing up in financially stable situations and growing up in government funded situations are polar opposite life experiences in the USA. In the hood safety is an anomaly, and no one experiences it regardless of their involvement in the street. If you are a resident of the ghetto, your odds skyrocket to be a victim of a crime. That ranges from elderly on down to babies. Bullets have no names. Some of the scariest nights growing up in the hood were days sleeping by my front door knowing someone could break in at any moment, and walking home through the projects to my house knowing I could get jumped, robbed, or worse at any time. Getting into fights or seeing shootings were things that I considered natural occurrences. Making it out the hood is one of the toughest tasks in society, and was my main goal in life. For most of my life I was always sympathetic for myself because of what I endured growing up in that environment. I had it worse than the majority of people I knew that grew up in the projects. By thinking with a local mindset, I felt I had it worse than anyone in the world. After meeting Hassan, I no longer felt that way.

I vented about things to Hassan that I felt were extreme growing up, such as not having a bathroom in my house for several years and witnessing murders as a youth. Those trials and tribulations were less extreme than what Hassan experienced. Ironically, many of his comparisons were similar situations, but were four times worse. As a child Hassan went four consecutive years without a consistent roof over his head. Here I was worried about someone breaking into my house, when Hassan did not even have a house to break into. During that time his family had to pitch tints in random places in the village or the wild on any given night. There was also a war going on in his country. Therefore violence was more extreme than what I could ever imagine. He had also witnessed murders growing up. The worse one was witnessing a man's head getting chopped off with a machete. The victim's head rolled near his shoes. During a war life still goes on for the citizens of that country. You still have to continue to educate yourself and provide during a war. After meeting him I became more appreciative for the simple things I took for granted.

Needless to say, he was beyond impressed by the steakhouse. I didn't take into account that Hassan had never been to a restaurant like this before. Hassan felt I introduced him to a new life that night. We did not spend much time at the restaurant discussing business. Mostly we cherished his first time in a fine steakhouse and discussed how we could make it out. The admiration and respect that Hassan showed me that night was the beginning of a new addiction. Not many things I came across in life were worth getting addicted to. Basketball was an addiction until I played in college. Playing in the amateur ranks from high school on down was not comparable to playing in college. In college you have to deal with politics, business, and financial challenges. Playing time is not always determined by who is the best player at that position. Other factors are taking into consideration such as if a players parents donate money to the institution, the ranking of the recruit even if he isn't playing up to standard, and off the book promises made by the coach to get a player to commit to the university. A student athlete from a financially stable family will have an entirely different experience of being a student athlete in college versus a student athlete coming from a poverty stricken home. To say being a college athlete is a full time job is an understatement. It is more than a full time job. When you are employed at a full-time job odds are you do not expose your body to severe injury every day, and chances are, you don't have to eat or train a certain way to keep your job. Collegiate athletes still have to eat, and train a certain way even when they aren't in season. Not many full time jobs will physically drain you then require you to do homework almost every night. The time consumption of having to be a performing athlete plus a performing student leaves you with very minimal time to make legal money. A college athlete from a financially stable family can expect money to be deposited in their bank account by their family or a savings account funded by their family. Many people come down on broke college athletes for doing illegal activities such as selling drugs, selling autographs, or accepting money from fans, but few people come up with ways, programs, or ideas to help these financially poor student athletes with their finances. Poor student athletes who are not on scholarships have it the absolute worse. They are even more at a disadvantage because they have to pay for school and will likely accumulate debt that will cripple them financially. After

20

experiencing what it was like to be a broke college athlete who was not headed to the NBA, I was no longer addicted to basketball. A common void that is mutual amongst most people who are unfulfilled is not having something they are passionate about. When basketball was taken from me I lost the only thing that I had a passion for. I felt as if I had lost my passion for life also. I did not care about getting killed or going to jail. I only got joy from getting respect and money in the streets. I found my new addiction.

I received a promotion in the streets after adding Hassan to my operation. The prior month I was just a street runner. No one answered to me or asked my opinion about any move and now I had a person who did. For two weeks straight Hassan and I sold three times more than I could have by myself and we continued to ask for more when we re'ed up. Uriah told me he would cut me off if I involved Bianca with business. I continued to keep my partnership with him and Derrick independent, and I also kept my workings with Hassan under wraps. No need for them to know how I got my job done as long as I got it done. Hassan also agreed it was time to add more people to our operation. We were moving around to too many places too often and became consistent faces in the wrong places. The idea of hiring Hassan was fifty times easier than the next decision I would have to make by adding a few new people to the operation. Hassan was trustworthy which was the most important trait to have. The hood was filled with hungry dogs, but then again. How loyal were hungry dogs? We went on a recruiting trip like we were college coaches or talent recruiters at a fortune 500 company.

I met Hassan on the porch for our daily routine on Thursday morning, and I figured that this would be the perfect day to figure out who I was going to add to my operation because I had to give Uriah his car back for the day. Caron, Tyrone, and Reggie, were three younger guys who stayed in the neighborhood that came to score from me almost every morning. Reggie did not fit in with Caron, and Tyrone. He was very sheltered and timid which are not great qualities to have in the streets. He began hanging with Caron and Tyrone after his father passed away. Tyrone and Caron used Reggie for his money and he was their crash dummy. Caron was the obvious leader of the clique and Tyrone was a perfect sidekick for him. They were loyal customers so I asked them to match one with me and Hassan. Caron responded with all of his chest out and said, "No we can't match one with you." I was astounded that he denied my overzealous invitation. Something didn't sit right with the way he said no. I asked why because I felt it was a reason behind the no that he failed to mention. Caron put his chest back in and tilted his head down and said, "We have to sell all of this and split the bread three ways." That statement notified me that I had an intermediate interview in front my face. I asked them to sit down I'll roll up three, one for each of them. After picking their brain for an hour I decided to put them on. Many people have extremely great aspirations in life but have very poor planning and execution. For example, many people want to lose weight or gain muscles, but they do not know the most effective workouts or diets to accomplish their goals. The goals Caron, Tyrone, and Reggie had were things that I had recently accomplished. Over the first month of their tenure I noticed I began to take a little more liking to Caron because he was never scared to speak his mind. He took advantage of my knowledge by picking my brain as much as possible, and he was the obvious leader of the group. In a little over three months, the group who used to walk the street with sno-ball stains on their dingy white t-shirts that had loose collars around the neck, and rarely got haircuts had graduated to purchasing nice cars, wearing different designer clothes every day, and maintained fresh haircuts. It would have been nice to have that disposable money also but all of my money went towards my tuition.

Caron texted me early Friday morning and asked could he take me to dinner later that night. It was so crazy that my time of being a student of Uriah came full circle. I knew it was about business, and he used one of my favorite learned tactics on me, talking business over some dinner. I had a jam packed day but I found a way to maneuver a few things around and agreed to have dinner with him. Wondering exactly what he wanted to meet about remained on my mind the entire day. It stayed on my mind during class, lunch with my father, sex with my girl, and my workouts which were usually events that captured my undivided attention. Despite taking a liking towards Caron I could not fully trust him.

After pulling up to the address he sent to me I noticed that it was a po-boy spot in the hood on the other side of town. It was very similar to the place where I bumped into my girlfriend for the first time since high school. Caron had the same level of respect at the po-boy shop as Uriah had at the steakhouse. It was encouraging to see so, but I was suspicious about why he had this deep of a connection with a hood on the other side of town. Katrina played a big role in displacing people from areas of the city that they grew up in so I could not jump to conclusions about him setting up shop in another neighborhood other than where he currently lived. It goes without saying that drug dealers are some of the most territorial people on earth. I had no choice but to get to the bottom of why he is set up shop there. The employees knew to cater to me and Caron on a different level. They cooked us food that wasn't on the menu and gave us our own private area to discuss business. As soon as we sat down Caron hunched over the table and said, "I need more. Reggie and Tyrone are holding me up. They are slowing down my time on re-ing up and it is costing me money that I desperately need. I set up shop here a few weeks ago because the owner was my park ball coach and all I have to do is give him minimal kickback. I can't grow my operation like this." As Caron began to vent I thought about being in the same situation with Brandon. I didn't even notice I left him behind until Caron brought up his situation with Reggie and Tyrone. I wish he could have kept up with me because I needed another person I could trust. After hearing Caron out I pushed for him to leave his crew behind. On Caron wanting more, I agreed to front him more but I could tell that it wasn't enough. He didn't speak on it so I left it where it was at. This happening made me realize I needed to tighten up my operation and get more organized. I knew it was time to decide between Derrick and Uriah as my main supplier. I had no idea which way I would go, but I set Monday as the deadline to make a decision.

Chapter 4

I needed a little time away from everything that weekend to make a vital decision. I decided to link with my girl for the rest of the night. I loved that my girl was a home body such as myself. Hanging with her inside was the isolation I needed. Being with her made me feel like I was on an exotic vacation. When Bianca arrived at my house around nightfall she was adamant about going to Biloxi, Mississippi. Her being aggressive about spontaneously going somewhere last minute was unusual. Every event she wanted to go to she gave me a heads up, but this time she made it seem as if we had to go immediately. She made a few incentives for going that I couldn't resist so we packed up and hit the road.

For majority of the forty-five minute drive she kept her head in my lap, but instead of enjoying it like any normal person would, I could not stop thinking about the decision I would have to make soon. I also had a feeling that Caron and Spike was on a different type of time. Why would any drug dealer drive loud colored vehicles, and I just didn't fully trust Caron. I felt something in the air. After getting to our destination things got back to normal when I saw my girl in her candy apple red dress. Being out of town with her provoked unfelt emotions. For the first time in my life I felt free. Previously I always felt tied down to something, whether it was basketball, school, or the hood. It was a feeling I thirsted for on a daily basis. Growing up I always felt I was in a war zone and was uncertain I would make it out. Being a broke college athlete I felt an immense pressure to perform in the classroom and on the court while I had no money. Since I started hustling I had to watch my peripheral twenty-four seven and slept with a gun by my side every night. The fast money was not a fair compensation for my sanity. I even thought about dropping out of college but I was too close to graduating. Each hand to hand transaction was a risk of my life or freedom. That night I felt nothing but life. I didn't have to look over my shoulder at all, and didn't have to tote a gun. I had money and a beautiful woman on my arm.

The next morning was a new experience. Growing up I had not been past state lines besides to play basketball and to visit my oldest brother in Maryland. While most students went on spring break vacations in college, I could not. I was broke and I was too focused on basketball. I also didn't drink alcohol while I played basketball in college for competitive advantages, and I did not want to be around temptation anyway. I still had to do my morning smoke, but I had no porch to smoke on, so I got creative. One good thing about being from the ghetto is knowing how to improvise. I went to the bathroom and got the shower cap the hotel provided me and sealed the smoke detector with it. After I sealed the smoke alarm with the shower cap I turned on the television. I felt finessed after I checked all of the channels to realize that we only had basic local stations on the television in our room. I was an avid news watcher so I got over it quickly. I was halfway into my second blunt when I saw a lime green SUV behind a news reporter with the caption "Kingpin Derrick "Spike" Wallace ARRESTED ON 1ST DEGREE MURDER CHARGES". Next the camera showed him being shoved into a police car. When he looked at the camera I felt like we locked eyes. I did not know what the look meant from him, but I had a feeling that it was not the last time I would see him even though it seemed like he would not be free again.

25

The next thirty minutes felt like thirty days. I didn't know how to feel about Derrick. He embraced me with so much love, so it was hard for me to see him taking a life. I also didn't believe that everything prosecuted in the courts and reported by the media was true. After I processed that Derrick would be going to jail I realized two things. One, I didn't have to choose between him and Uriah, and two, I just came up a few thousand dollars because I didn't have to pay him back for the work he fronted me at the moment. I did not want to wake my girl up because I always want silence when I am soaking in life changing moments. I jumped in the shower and wondered about my next moves. I felt Derrick getting arrested was a sign for me to go all in with Uriah, but it's not like I had another choice. Tuition still needed to be paid and a job still hadn't called. As I stepped out of the shower I heard my girl's phone ring three times back to back to back like the Chicago Bulls in 1996. The sun had not come up yet so I figured it was important. I tried to wake her up but she was too tired to respond. When I reached to silence her phone I could not help but to read the words on the screen. The font seemed as big as letters on a billboard. I suddenly had the reading level of a third grader when I tried to read the message on the screen. U R I A H I S D E A D. As soon as I read the text my girl rubbed me on my back and asked me what I was doing. I never believed in opening someone's phone. You will find out whatever is hiding in that person's phone if it were meant to be. I quickly responded in the slowest manner, "Your uncle is dead bae." My girl laughed then took her phone from me, and casually opened it. When she read the message that her uncle is dead she began to swing at me and cry every drop of water out of her body. She acted as if I killed him. I felt like a vegetable on the inside. Derrick was headed to jail to fight a murder charge, and my other plug, which happened to be my girlfriend's uncle, was dead.

Bianca ferociously stormed out of the room, didn't take any of her belongings and left without saying goodbye. My whole world had been flipped upside down in twenty-four hours. It really hurts making the same mistake twice. One day a kid who I mentored father was killed and I immediately called him after I found out without taking into consideration what he was doing at the time. It was a horrible decision and terrible timing because he was around a lot of people when I told him. After I told him that news at such a poor time he never looked at me the same and our relationship was never what it once was before his father's death. We still got along, but he had subliminal anger towards me. As a child my dad told me it's not what you do, it's how you do it. He told me don't ever tell someone a tragic event in the middle of the day while they are around other people, and do not spring it on them. After realizing that I sprung tragic news on Bianca as soon as she woke up, I knew our relationship had died right along with Uriah. The three most important people in my life besides my family were all gone from me in a matter of one hour. I was on a roller coaster that took me from heaven to hell. We initially had the room for one night, but Bianca and I were no longer a we.

I was not ready to go back to the city that turned my heart from warm to cold. My first conscious memory of my childhood was a man getting killed not many feet away from me. The rest of my childhood from six years old until eleven years old I spent majority of my time falling in love with basketball, fighting, and learning every old school jam. I always knew every old school song backwards because I grew up across the street from a bar room that played music until 4:00am almost every morning. My adolescence was spent without household essentials. I had to pass my bowels in a bucket, because we did not have a toilet in the house. I stayed with a ring around my ass those years. I also stayed with shoulder pain because one night a bullet pierced through my bedroom window and cracked my television screen that was next to my head. After earning a scholarship to the most expensive school in Louisiana for middle school it had felt like a dream come true. My previous elementary school was some shit realer than you could imagine on a movie. Sixth graders were having sex at school, you had to jump over piss puddles to get to the urinal, and you had to be ready to fight every day like you were in the penitentiary. At my new school I was able to use the bathroom without jumping over puddles of urine, and the toilet was clean enough to sit on without toilet paper although I would never do such a trifling thing. I was so happy to be changing schools.

My nightmare began on the first day of school. I was looked at as if I were a UFO. There were no other children of color in my class. There was only one other black child in my grade so you know they had to split us up. My entire first day I was stared at and over analyzed. My wavy hair, different dialect, and different style of clothing were watched closely all day. People asked to touch my hair as if I were the main attraction at a petting zoo. I never knew what racism and being stereotyped was until that day. I was in a physically safe environment for the first time in life, but being in such a racist environment proved to be more dangerous and detrimental. I never knew how much a child's parent income helped determine the quality of education a child would receive. Not one person at my former elementary school parents could afford to send them to my new school. As a child I had to worry about things that were considered adult problems. I took that pain with me to my new school. I also bought that pain with me to my prior school but I was never provoked on a daily basis to unleash it. "Poor jokes" were the main genre of jokes at my new school. My reality was made fun of because no one could relate to the struggle. They also did not think a person who is actually from situations that they made fun of could be going to school with them. As I began to go against the grain on racist white supremacist views, teachers began to tell my parents that I needed psychiatric medicine to control my behavior. It was vomitous that teachers who had no medicinal training or licenses told my parents that I needed psychiatric medicine. It will forever hurt me that teachers who were paid to brighten my future tried to darken mines because they couldn't teach through our social differences to see my intellect.

After middle school ended I moved back to an all-black high school. I could not get past a 2.0 grade point average my freshman and sophomore year because I could not control myself being in an environment that I missed so much. I finally got back on track going into my junior year, but in 2005 Hurricane Katrina placed nine feet of water in my house destroying all of my memorabilia along with destroying the rest of my city. Pain from Katrina, my childhood, and my adolescence left me with a damaged heart, but I still had basketball. My basketball career until the age of fourteen years old I was always looked at as a solid player. I had defense, heart, handles, and was a good shooter. While I was a shooter, I was not mainly referred to as a scorer. Not being viewed for my strengths was problematic. That year I dedicated most of my time bettering my craft at the St. Bernard Center. I realized that fighting and hanging in the project for respect was a waste of time. I could not get a scholarship for respect in the hood, but I deserved one for it because of how hard it was to obtain it. My friend Ahyaro was already looked at as a legend in the project because he was gifted at basketball and was extremely intelligent. He guided me towards taking my game to the gym so we could improve our game enough to make it out. I was easily convinced. Being persuaded by him to go to the gym and after instantly earning respect there it took my game and confidence to new heights. From all of the love I received from other people in the gym I felt pressure and a sense of urgency to make it out and developed a mindset that no one could fuck with me. That led me and Ahyaro to using basketball to further our education at top universities which is almost unheard of for people from our hood. After I graduated from high school I visited my oldest brother in Maryland. The first two nights I stayed up watching porn, talking on the phone until the wee hours of the morning, and woke up in the afternoon. The third morning I was woken up with a fist in my chest and a missing phone. My brother's biggest gifts were his powerful voice, and his life changing words. He used that powerful voice in my face after he punched me and said, "You are a joke. Your short lazy ass has an opportunity to play basketball at a top university and you're going to sleep that chance away. There are people who are six foot five across the world who play your same position that have been getting up at five every morning to work on their game and you rather watch uncut instead of competing with them to be the best. Your local mindset of being the best person in the hood is going to put you right back in the hood." Ever since then I had a work ethic that could be put up against anyone in the world. For three years straight I got up every day at five in the morning five days a week to work on my craft, and it was all taken away because I decided to smoke the plant to ease my mind from all pain and stress I experienced my whole life. The NCAA couldn't understand everything I had been through, and neither could my athletic director, so I knew my basketball dreams were over. Eighteen years, ten thousand practices, five thousand early morning practices, countless injuries, countless times playing through them, countless blood and tears given to the game were all gone in the wind with a half blunt.

Chapter 5

I only had two months left to complete my college degree. I contemplated not going back to the city to finish even though I spent my whole life working towards achieving a college degree. I decided to extend my stay for one more night at the hotel. My intention was to figure out where to go from here, but my mind was in neutral. I couldn't get anywhere mentally. I did not move for food, water, or the plethora calls I missed. It was sanity damaging that life was still going on during a time of tragedy. People still had the nerve to call my phone to supply their habit while I went through immense pain and confusion. The same thing happened during every tragedy in life. When people die in life, bill collectors still call, offices of the deceased are immediately emptied out then filled with their replacement, and strangers still enjoy themselves in your presence. How could people still live while you were currently dying on the inside? The more you see in life, the more you become open to death. As you incur more mental pain, physical pain, and lose people you love, the closer you get to accepting your afterlife. However, the more love that enters your world such as the birth of a new life, or a spouse you love, you take more precautions to extend your life. After sobering up a little from the pain, I was motivated enough to head back home and face what the city had in store for me next.

When I got in the car at four in the morning I realized that Uriah wouldn't be asking for his car back. I didn't necessarily know how the legal process went on that, but I knew I was not giving the car back. I was usually a slow driver because of the way my dad taught me how to drive, but that morning I had more on my mind besides driving. I was ahead of schedule on the way back. I had made thirty minutes progress in fifteen minutes. As I reached down to turn the radio on to listen to my favorite singer Greg Banks, it felt as if someone had shot out my passenger's side front tire after I got over the hump of the bridge that was surrounded by a lake. I previously lost a friend from him overcorrecting his vehicle when he lost control. After I lost control of the car I panicked. I saw my deceased friend for the first time since I saw him lay in the coffin at his funeral. His face made an appearance on my windshield. My adrenalin ceased after I saw him and I was able to control the whip with both hands. Going downhill only made the car go faster, but my dead friend guided me safely down the bridge onto a rest stop which was not far from the foot of the bridge. After the car stopped my heart lifted out of my feet back up to my chest. Being shook up from seeing my dead friend on my windshield, and losing control of my car while going downhill made me sit still for a few minutes so I could gather myself. This was the first time I ever had to go in the trunk of Uriah's old car. For some reason I was always paranoid about going in any compartment in the car, whether it was the glove compartment, the side pockets, the middle console, or the trunk. I didn't even know how to pop the trunk on this fancy ass car. I had no choice but to hurry up and figure it out so I could fix the flat on the side of the road in the wee hours of the morning. My beautiful dark skin and the foreign car I drove made me a police magnet. The trunk was easier to pop than what I expected. The inside of the trunk looked as clean as if it were still sitting at the dealership. The new car smell graced my lungs and made me think of how professional and organized Uriah was. When I peeled back the cover of the trunk floor, there were two layers of sturdy cardboard covering where the spare was. That wasn't an obstacle. Every day since I was fifteen years old I kept a pocket knife in my jeans for a sense of peace and protection. I had more pocket knives than belts. I finally had a reason to use my knife that I carried every day. I pulled the trunk cover out and dug my blade into the pieces of cardboard and dragged it the entire length of the trunk. White and beige residue covered my wrist and hand.

I pulled the cardboard out in the most animalistic manner. Tightly wrapped bags of white and beige powder covered the spare tire. I was never face to face with cocaine before but I knew exactly what it was. In every movie I saw, when a drug dealer first got some new cocaine the first thing they did was taste it for quality. I did just that, and my tongue felt like it evaporated in my mouth. I knew it was great. I had to make so many life altering decisions in the past few months, and failed miserably at the last one. I was so ready to make another life changing decision and here was one sitting in my trunk. I was so anxious to make the right move with the drugs I just found. Caron wanted more and this was the way I could deliver more on his plate. I had no intention of selling cocaine and heroin before I opened the trunk, but I knew it was a package that I could not donate. I did not know how to sell cocaine or heroin, but great thing Hassan did. I changed the tire quicker than anyone in tire-shop history and got back on the road.

I had two calls to make on the way home. Hassan to make sure he was down for our morning ritual, and Caron to see if he was ready for the more that he was looking for. I was beyond excited to be able provide the more that Caron said he wanted so quick and unexpectedly. I didn't know exactly what he meant when he said he wanted more, but I felt this had to be what he insinuated. I felt I would gain his loyalty for life if I were able to come through for him and one day I would be able to smoothly pass the game on to him when I was ready to exit it. I never thought about a succession plan until after the prior weekend. I knew at the end of each gangster movie there was never a happy ending for the drug dealer. The heroes who I viewed upon in that light both Uriah and Derrick had fell victim to the two most popular casualties in the streets, murdered and jailed. Before I felt that new perspective of love with Bianca the previous Friday night, I didn't care about getting killed or going to jail. Hell couldn't be much worse than what I was living through. When I first met Hassan he slightly changed my mind about that, but things only got darker progressively as life went on. I did not have a compassion for life. I never understood how so many great people with hearts of gold were born into a life of struggle and how so many crooked people were born into heavenly conditions. After experiencing both financial spectrums in life, I realized that some of the happiest people were financially broke, and some of the most depressed people were rich. People who are born into poverty have more of an appreciation for simple things in life. Lights would be appreciated more if you grew up in a situation where they were cut off periodically, and you had to light your house with candles. Accomplishments are celebrated harder when you grew up around the unaccomplished. Relationships are more sacred if you knew that you could have a friend who would kill or rob you for the right price.

I called Caron before the sun could come up and it sounded like he was deep into the middle of his day already. I called to tell Caron what happened because I had another 30 minutes

33

il. As I told him what happened to Derrick and Uriah he ᵢmed unconcerned and didn't express any condolences for ᵢm. Caron said, "I had heard of the both of them but that's the life they chose. That was just the play that life had for them. It's time to take their customers and territories." I agreed, but I felt a weird vibe because he didn't express any sympathy for them and he knew my relationship with Uriah and Derrick. I had to realize that I was in the streets, and ain't no love in them. Especially for people that didn't know each other. When I told Caron the price I was thinking of charging him for what I found in Uriah's trunk he didn't flinch like I expected him to. I was expecting negotiation from him being that it was a price triple of anything he had purchased from me. He agreed to the price as if it were only ten dollars. I asked what time and where, and he responded "At my spot for 7:00pm. Things must be great on that end huh. I need to get like you. I am going to catch you later big homie." then hung up. Caron broke into happiness as if he had hit the lottery and I had never even seen him smile before.

I made it right in time for my daily morning joce with Hassan. I hadn't called Hassan to tell him anything that happened during the past weekend. All I could do was think about getting rid of this twenty-five year prison sentence in my trunk. I rolled up a blunt while I was driving so I could get straight to the point with Hassan when I made it back home. Usually each move I made in the game since I bought Hassan on board full time I consulted with him prior to the move. This morning wasn't a consultation. I had a plan that I was rolling out. I just needed to know what was the appropriate amount to charge, and if he was down. After I lit up, I told Hassan I had a trunkful of cocaine and heroin, not how I got it, or where I got it from. He didn't ask where I got it from, just why? I told him I stumbled on a package from God, and that's our sign more money is on the way. I never considered it to be from the Devil. Hassan said we needed to sell it ASAP, but we should break it down and sell it. I wanted to move it all at once. He disagreed, but still went with my plan. We assessed the value and it was time to make a move. Hassan said he knew four people that would be down to buy it by the end of the week. I said I knew one person that would buy it tonight. Let's go make this move by Caron tonight and get off of it. Hassan said, "I know you fucking lying. That's the last person we need to sell to. You know he doesn't give a fuck and would turn on us for the money. Plus I know he doesn't even have the money." I took a deep breath and said "Hassan, he has the money. The only reason he keeps Reggie around is because his dad just passed and left him a lot of money and Reggie didn't mind spending it on being Caron's flunky. Plus Caron looks up to us so he wouldn't make a false move."

As I watched the sunrise, it finally set in that Uriah wouldn't live to see it and Derrick wouldn't see it from behind bars. I had finally got into another routine in life and it was uprooted again. Hurricane Katrina had hit more than once in my life. I finally felt in charge as if I were the main plug. That was a misconception though. No one should ever refer to themselves as the plug in the streets because there is always someone higher. It is an everlasting hierarchy. Nonetheless, it was another promotion in the streets. It was two less people above me and I could provide more work for the people below me. I just had to find out who Derrick and Uriah's plugs were. I knew going forward shit would get realer than I could imagine, so I decided I wanted to just kick back and enjoy the day with my brother Hassan until it was time to meet up with Caron.

That past Friday was the first time I did anything to enjoy the fruits of my labor. It gave me a rush to finally not have to check my balance when I made purchases. It also felt good having my ass kissed at places I would usually not be welcomed in. I wanted those feelings again today. We decided to parlay in Hassan's car since mine had felony charges in the trunk. Hassan was the first friend of mines with a car growing up. He purchased a car when he made seventeen years old. It was still late compared to most other kids in high school, but it stopped us from catching the bus and walking everywhere. I always felt as if I were riding in a foreign car in high school when I rode with him. After being in a foreign car I finally saw Hassan's car for what it really was a hooptee. Riding with him that day reminded me of how much we had been through together and it gave me a deeper appreciation for his friendship. Hassan and I always rode with each other no matter what the ride was like. I was always frugal with my money, but who am I to kid? I never had money until I started hustling. I felt spending money would make me want to work even harder to make more. I looked at it as an investment. Hassan asked what I wanted to eat for breakfast as we pulled off in his car that sounded like a lawnmower in dire need an oil change. I responded, "I don't know what I want to eat, but let's pull up at the mall and get something new to wear to go to breakfast." When people who never had money before finally obtain some, they usually make irrational decisions when it comes to spending their new found money. It is a challenge to be financially literate when you grew up poor.

Hassan was a little different from the average US born citizen. Majority of the time when people offer someone food, money, or a favor when they are not required to, most people would shy away from accepting. Not Hassan, he planned out his entire outfit and did not stop talking about it until we got to the mall. I began looking through my phone as he continued to ramble. I logged into my social media accounts for the first time in almost a year. I couldn't believe my last post date. I saw what people meant when they said, real hustlers of the streets aren't on social media. It was a sense of discretion that I needed to move with knowing I could draw attention that could be detrimental to my freedom and existence. What I was risking everyday was too real to interact with social media.

I wanted a mixture of Derrick's and Uriah's style. I wanted the sense of fashion Derrick possessed, and the professionalism and business mindset of Uriah. It was time to show the world what I had grown into and for them to say hello to the new me. "I am back." was what I posted. I put my phone down after that, and Hassan was still rambling so I decided to pick it back up. I had over fifty notifications, and one of them was a friend request. The friend request caught my eye because it was a beautiful woman who I never seen before. I thought I had seen every gorgeous woman in the city before but obviously I had not. I was excited to see faces I hadn't seen in forever, and to see people express their different points of views. Most of all I missed laughing. There wasn't much I had to laugh about during the past year. A smile that was once on display everyday was buried under a heart so cold. The social media appearance was a tease. I knew I was not back like I posted I was. As we pulled into the parking lot of the mall I slid lower in my seat so no one could see me as I rode in Hassan's car. I felt two eyes looking at me with their undivided attention but I did not want to make eye contact with anyone while I was looking stupid sliding down the passenger seat. It was her. It was her! The girl who sent me the friend request. We locked eyes as my face sunk to the bottom of the window until I was out of sight.

When we walked through the doors it was a feeling of oasis. My mom always took me to window shop at Saks growing up, but I finally had the money to purchase whatever I wanted. Hassan shared the same excitement. Within the first thirty seconds of standing in the store, five people aggressively approached us and asked if we needed help. I always felt out of place in environments like this because of my experiences in middle school. I thought money would give me acceptance in these environments, but I couldn't be more wrong. The unofficial security guards did not stop our fun though. The price tags made me tentative to buy anything because I never spent that much money on apparel before. Even a pair of socks. Hassan wanted to try on everything in the store so I really had some time to shop around. I didn't even know how to shop in a store that didn't have a clearance rack. The clearance racks were the first and last areas I searched for

37

anytime I went shopping, and this store did not have one. A table of Burberry attire near the escalator caught my eyes. I knew Burberry was expensive, but I never actually knew how much. I approached the table as if it were a final exam I didn't study for. When I got to the table I saw the girl who sent me a friend request again on the floor below me with her back turned. She had to feel my energy because she turned around as soon as I spotted her. I dropped my head and looked at whatever was in arms reach as she watched me. A price tag was the closest thing I could look at to play it off. My interest in the price tag became falsely intensified. When I read the price tag, the Oscar deserved to go to me for not making a facial expression or body gesture towards the price. I had no option but to buy the clothes. I gathered a few items in my size and headed to the register. I barked at Hassan, "Stop being a fuckin model and let's get out of here", as if someone was after me.

As we rode to breakfast I felt like the biggest bitch in the world because I did not approach her when the opportunity presented itself. I accomplished everything I sat out to do, but froze at the chance to embark on an unexpected opportunity. That taught me a life lesson. Underachieving is one of the worst feelings in the world. Sometimes en route to achieving your goals an unexpected opportunity could appear simultaneously that may be bigger than your original goals. What you once thought was overachieving should be looked at as underachieving in that situation if you do not capitalize on the unexpected opportunity. I am glad Hassan was too caught up in the moment to pry at why I was acting different that morning. We got dressed in the parking lot when we arrived at the restaurant. It was obvious we never purchased clothes for a same day event because we didn't even think to get dressed in the dressing room where we bought the clothes at. It weighed on my mind each minute that I froze up when I had the opportunity to meet such a beautiful woman. That low cancelled out any high I could have felt.

Fifty calls were missed over the prior weekend while I was out of town. It had to double after getting back on social media. It was hard for me to open my phone without my new love interest's phone number in my contacts. Since I hadn't told Hassan the whole story about what happened yet, breakfast seemed like perfect timing to let him know what went down. Hassan was one of the best people to tell a story to. He gave you his undivided attention and his interaction after every pause adds more unplanned suspense to the story. I had to use the restroom since we walked into the shopping center so after I finished the story about what happened the prior weekend I made way to the restroom. I checked my phone as I walked to the restroom. I knew most of my calls and texts were from people who were trying to score, so I only checked social media. I had a direct message and it was from her. "Hey, I think I just saw you at the mall. Did you have a black shirt and black jeans on?" I wrote back, "Yes that was me. I wish I would have seen you." I almost dropped the phone when she replied back, "You can see me later today if you want, "504-555-1234" I jogged back to the table and told Hassan, "We have to dip asap. I have to see my uncle before he leaves town." I told him that so he wouldn't ask to come along after we got back to the house. I knew exactly what I was going to wear, but didn't know exactly where to take her, or what to say once we got there. When Hassan and I got back to our house we moved the twenty-five year prison sentence from my trunk to his trunk. I wondered was it a good idea to take her to the steakhouse that Uriah had turned me onto. I decided that could have been the dumbest idea I could have come up with. I had a meeting with Caron that same night on his side of town so I decided to take her to a steakhouse in that area.

Later that night when I pulled up at my date's house I called Caron twice while I waited for her to come outside but he didn't answer. When she got in the car it was a presence that I never felt before. After she sat down I felt a rush of energy, confidence, and motivation to be the epitome of a man. She garnered my undivided attention immediately. Conversation came easy and we vibed as if we had known each other our entire lives. As we got closer to the other side of the city it dawned on me that Caron had not hit me back yet. We posted up outside of Caron's place of business for twenty minutes. She asked what are we doing here and I told her I wanted to see my uncle before he left town. I couldn't believe I lied to Hassan and her so easily. Were both of those truths worth lying about? After about twenty-five minutes of sitting there I decided to pull off. New Orleans has a thing about having hoods and nice neighborhoods only blocks apart from each other. The steakhouse where we were going was only nine blocks away. I texted Caron to let him know that I was pulling off from his spot. He called me before I could close my phone. Caron said he was in the hospital and apologized for not keeping me in the loop. I couldn't deal with more pain so I didn't ask him why he was there. He also didn't sound like anything too tragic happened. I expressed my condolences and told him to holler at me later. As we rode to the steakhouse I noticed a car was trailing a few blocks behind us. The car made every turn I made. It was too far back to be a jacker, it had to be undercovers. I knew Caron was generating too much traffic in this area. It made me feel comfortable that Caron did a lot of things that reminded him of me, but him flaking on me was not something that reminded me of myself. Disrespecting someone's time is the most disrespectful thing you could do. It is one thing if you are late or miscommunications happen once you arrive, but to not show up at all is a slap in the face. A person could never get back the time that was wasted.

When we got to the steakhouse it was not the same level of love I received at the place I normally did business at, but it was similar. After I pulled up in a foreign car and well fitted high end designer clothing I was a welcomed customer. People always say dress as you want to be perceived, but why should I have to wear clothes that conform to the stereotypical norm to avoid being negatively stereotyped?

When I am dressed in attire such as a baseball hat, sweatpants, or a plain t-shirt I am usually negatively stereotyped. Black men in non-formal clothes are looked at as physical threats. Black men in formal clothes are looked at as mental threats. My date and I enjoyed everything on the menu that we desired and the entire dinner went perfect. I had the magical feeling of where have you been my entire life. After dinner we went to a quiet lounge so we could get to know each other better in a more intimate setting. I was hornswoggled that Lisa had been through so much. She lost her dad before she was born and her mom died a year later. She bounced around from foster home to foster home in New York, and finally moved back to the city where she was born. Despite having been through so much her smile would lead you to believe her life was perfect. Her trials and tribulations gave me new life knowing she had been through so many tragic things and was still able to be so happy. I felt silly bringing up my struggles in life after hearing hers. I wanted to tell her what I was going through, but I didn't want to take any chance of losing her due to my lifestyle. I went the entire night without bringing it up. My mind began to race while I waited for her to walk inside her house. I began to regret taking her with me to meet Caron. How could I take someone who I liked so much with me on a mission that could land me in jail or dead? She grew up in the hood, many hoods at that, but she was different than most women from there. She didn't see herself as her environment, and limit herself to that. My ex and other women whom I came across over the past year celebrated that I hustled and it turned them on. I was not sure if Lisa would like that. Let alone even continue to talk to me after she found out I sold drugs. Could a woman really love you if she pushed you to be in the streets?

That question made me think about my childhood barber, Bird. He and his girl Sunny were Bonnie and Clyde before I knew who the real Bonnie and Clyde were. They made me hate when people are overly sexual in public. Bird and Sunny kissed over my head so many times over the years that Bird was responsible for giving me the freshest light fade in New Orleans. Sunny always ran Bird's drugs in and out of the shop and the city. They never disrespected each other and the only disagreement I saw was when Bird got a job offer that would have paid more money than cutting hair and hustling combined, but Sunny made him turn the job offer down. Bird saw more for himself than cutting hair and hustling but he sacrificed it to please Sunny. One day when I got suspended within the first hour of being at school my dad sent Bird to pick me up because he was the only available option to scoop me up that early unexpectedly. Bird and Sunny spent that entire day pretending as if I was their son. That situation made me want the day to never end. This was the first time I had been under the supervision of a couple who were in love. That one day stuck with me for the rest of my life. Being spoiled by a couple who were in love was a dream to me as a child. It wasn't even really about going out to eat every time I was hungry, and buying me gifts. It was just about being in the presence of two people who were in love that I enjoyed so much.

A week later, when it was time to go back to the barbershop I had to travel by foot. Bird or my dad usually gave me a ride to the shop, but both of them were out of town. The barbershop was two miles away from my house. I decided to stop at the levee to use the bathroom. The levee was a duck off spot for grownups to have sex and smoke. The sun was going down by the time I got to the levee. Only one car was parked at the secluded location. It looked as if it was John Perrymount's car. He went to Georgetown on a full scholarship in the late 80's and became a popular drug dealer in Washington DC. He came home on occasion, but everyone still knew him back home because of his legendary status in the streets and basketball. I didn't know much about sex at the age of nine, but I knew it had to be going on in his car by the way his car explosively rocked up and down. I maneuvered throughout the bushes so I could watch without being seen. When I finally got a great view, all I saw was some beautiful titties with hoop earrings on them, a flat stomach with defined abs, and Sunny's face.

I laid on the ground and cried until they pulled off. My perspective of love was dismantled. Growing up in a non-dual parent household makes you wonder if your being wasn't a good enough reason for your parents to stay together. I questioned my importance to my parents many times growing up because of so. After I saw that there are things that go on in relationships behind closed doors, I knew the traditional approach was not always the best option for everyone. Watching Sunny on top of another man while she pretended to be in love with Bird broke my heart more than it could have broken Bird's heart if he found out. They were the only couple that I looked up to as a child. Previously, I got a haircut every week, but to avoid slipping up and saying something to Bird about Sunny I went the next two months without getting a haircut. I dealt with jokes from everyone about my hairline, but they were worth taking on the chin for Bird. I decided to finally get a haircut after my last basketball game of the year. I got a ride to the barbershop from my coach instead of Bird because I wanted to be around him as limited amount of time as possible to increase my chances of not saying anything. When I got in the barbershop it was a slow walk towards my barber's chair. His back was turned to the door when I entered the shop. As I approached Bird he spun his chair around and guess who was sitting in his chair? None other than John Perrymount. Bird pointed at me and said, "That's my boy right there Perrymount. He is going to be the next you one day. He plays the game with so much heart and has a left hand just like you". Perrymount was so graceful and smooth that he made me forget everything I saw when him and Sunny was fucking. I felt five times smoother and better after I talked to him. He had such a captivating style and a broad vocabulary as if he had a thesaurus in front of him while he talked. I sat down and didn't say anything as if I owed loyalty to Perrymount for holding that secret. After Bird had finished tightening up his fade Sunny walked up. Bird had the same excitement to introduce Perrymount to his girlfriend as he did when he introduced me to him. If he only knew how well they had already been introduced. Bird bragged on him to Sunny and said Perrymount was one of the best basketball players ever and one of the best people he knew. Sunny obviously felt the same way, but she acted as if he was nothing and they had never met before.

The following morning around daybreak I went back to the barbershop because I left my headband that I had been using to cover up my lining for the past two months by Bird's barber station. I had no use for it, but my mom spent her last money to buy it for me so it was urgent that I retrieved it. Bird was known for his ritual of getting to the barbershop before daybreak. I figured I would impress him by beating him there that morning. I had to stop at the duck off along the way because I forgot to use the bathroom after I woke up like any normal person does. It felt great not having flashbacks of laying on the ground crying while I watched Sunny and Perrymount on the levee knocking boots. As I walked to the barbershop I became a little nervous because of the fog. I knew something could go down and it was a high chance that no one would witness it. I was two blocks away when I saw Bird get out of his car to open the barbershop. It seemed as if he had walked across a football field due to how long it took him to get to the front door of the shop. I heard brakes squeak that sounded similar to Sunny's car in the block between me and Bird. A tall slender guy appeared on the corner in between us and then checked his surroundings. My heart dropped to my shoelaces when I thought he spotted me but the fog and a pickup truck kept me from being visible. After the tall guy who resembled Perrymount saw that the coast was clear he crept up behind Bird before Bird could turn around and let three shots off in his back. The bullets turned Bird around then the gunman stood over Bird and emptied the clip into his body. Sunny's car briskly turned the block and the murderer jumped in the car and they pulled off into the thick morning fog.

44

I had witnessed my second murder before the tender age of ten. My want for love was killed along with Bird. My first heartbreak came by indirect contact. I was heartbroken after I saw Sunny fuck John then I became heartless when she moved on with her boyfriend's killer. Sunny and John started a family, got married, and then moved to DC. Sunny was like most women who encouraged their men to live the street life. The most disgusting thing about those types of women was that if their lover got arrested, or killed they would be on to the next person before their man was laid six feet deep. Sometimes the next person that they moved on with was the person responsible for their previous lover's death or jail time.

Chapter 6

On the memorable ride home after I dropped Lisa off I decided I would tell her about my secret life once we got on the phone later that night. As soon as I made it back home we talked on the phone until she got sleepy. I could tell our conversation was about to come to a close, and I thought I dodged the bullet of not having to tell her I sold drugs until she said, "One more question before I go to sleep. What do you do for a living? You stay in the hood but have a foreign car, thousand dollar outfits, and can afford $200 dates, but you never go to work." Being prepared for the conversation I quickly responded, "I hustle." "Hustle what?" she asked. My voice lowered and said, "I sell weed." Her voice intensified as she asked, "Are you sure that is all you sell?" I said, "Yes" with an obvious level of uncertainty because I knew I had cocaine and heroin to sell. Lisa hung up in my face after I answered yes. I cringed because she took it way worse than I expected. I presented myself as something different. I made her fall in love with my ambition to make it out by legal plans, and I hid my love for the streets during conversations with her. The rest of that night was supposed to be spent making plans adjusting to life without Derrick and Uriah, but I could not take my mind off my new found love. I never thought of losing her as an option. I just had to open up to her so she could fall in love with the real me, and not who she assumed I was. I decided to write my feelings down on paper and place it in her mailbox before the sun came up the next morning.

Hassan was at work the next morning so I decided to stay in bed during our normal meeting time. After seeing Derrick on the television I was reluctant to watch the news but that was a better option than going back to sleep. I was on edge to see what was next in life. Uriah's funeral was Friday and I was not ready to see him go six feet deep. I didn't think Derrick would reach out to me behind bars due to how low I was in his organization but I had to keep some money on the side just in case he wanted the money back that I owed him from when he fronted me. Defense attorneys don't come cheap. I wondered who could have Derrick killed. He seemed as the delegating type when it was time for physical enforcement. Someone must have tried to rob him. That's the only way I could see him killing someone. Uriah didn't seem like a person to draw a lot of heat on himself. His fate was somewhat hard to fathom also. If you looked at him, he looked like someone who sold breath mints in the restroom at a club. He had expensive garments, but wore them poorly. He never cared to iron his shirt, or brush his hair, so he always had cuckleberries in his head. Uriah's hair was tougher than a three dollar steak. His explanation was that he hated attention, but hated the way cheap clothes felt against his skin. Every time someone dies I always make it imperative to incorporate their great qualities in myself so they live on through me. I picked up so much game from them both and looked forward to them grooming me as I developed in the game. Their loss was a pain that chilled my heart and left me with no guidance in the streets.

The letter I left Lisa started the week off with great

momentum. I always looked at Monday as the best day of the week. Mondays are the most challenging day of the week for most people because they do not rest properly and fully prepare to take on a day full of activities that are more intense than their weekend activities. Mondays are the biggest mind-fuck in society. How could you not look forward to another day in life? I never understood why people bitched up for Monday. After she read the letter it was no looking back from my confession. The confession seemed to put everything behind us, but I could tell there was an elephant in the room when I was with her. Her energy was stronger than words. Her body language spoke above a yell but as gentle as a whisper.

I had done more running than ever that week. I had to keep switching cars with Hassan and visited Lisa whenever I wasn't making moves. I never involved her in anything that would put her in harm's way. My last situation was the opposite. Bianca was there for almost every move I made in the streets. I thought she was there because of her love for me, but she was just there for her love of the streets. The streets made us feel alive because we were dead on the inside. Lisa made me feel alive again. Thinking about seeing Bianca at Uriah's funeral was the first time another woman crossed my mind since Lisa came into my life. Even though Bianca crossed my mind, my feelings for her were as dead as Uriah.

Most of my weed was sold and I still had not found a connect. It was time to focus on getting off the rest of the narcotics. Caron pushed our meeting back until the night of the funeral. Usually a deal like this would be pushed up instead of backwards. I was too caught up in getting to know Lisa to worry about what he was on. It was time for Uriah's funeral. My girl had slept by me that Thursday night and knew about the funeral Friday morning but did not offer to come with me. I was surprised that she did not ask. This was the first time there was a disconnect in our relationship from my end. I felt she did not respect my relationship with Uriah because I met him in the streets. Was I fooling myself that a woman like that could ever fall for someone like me? After I dropped Lisa off at her house on Friday morning before Uriah's funeral my mind drifted back towards seeing Bianca. I realized that she did not have many close people in her family besides Uriah and I might have to step up and still be there for her regardless of her having a strong resentment for me.

When I arrived to the funeral it looked like the stereotypical funeral of a kingpin. There were plenty of women in the mega church who had all seemed to have lost their husband. Other kingpins of every culture were there. The Italians, the Mexicans, and the crooked white collar gangsters were all there. The only group that seemed to be missing was young black gangsters. The diversity amongst drug lords made me realize the importance of networking with different cultures. As I stood by the doors of the church I realized that I was early but the seats appeared full. Uriah was always an hour early for everything so it was only right to be an hour early for his funeral. As I scanned the premises for a seat, two men the size of professional football linemen walked from the front of the church in my direction. As they walked towards me I remembered that I still had Uriah's car in my possession and his drugs. They guided me to the front of the church. My ex was in the seat that usually a wife or the mother sits of the deceased man. I was in the seat where the father or husband of the deceased usually sits.

I was bamboozled at my acknowledgment at the services. I never heard of a funeral where someone who the deceased person met the same year they passed had a seat reserved for them on the front row at their funeral. My relationship with Uriah and his niece was better known than what I previously assumed before the funeral. From the looks of it Bianca and I appeared to be married at the funeral. Throughout the services I consoled my ex the entire time. I could not believe we could get this close after I thought our relationship was over. I was still unsure if that was the last time I would hold her in my arms again. Uriah's funeral was an open coffin however it should not have been. He looked like a wax dummy as he lay in the coffin. It was amazing that he got shot in the face three times and still had an open coffin. He was a tough muthafucka. I had to carry my ex to the limousine. A limo usually rides eight people from the church to the cematary however only Bianca and myself rode in the limo to Uriah's gravesite. She cried her tears out on my suit and kept her arms draped around me the entire ride. Her energy told me that she needed me and I was all she had left. When we got to the graveyard, my ex's friends took over consoling her. The same men who guided me from the back of the church to the front asked me to follow them as soon as Bianca walked off.

I followed the grizzly bear built men to a van that could easily be mistaken for a kidnappers van. The sketchy van was filled with all of the kingpins whom I saw in the church. If you let the USA tell it, you would think all the gangsters in the country were black and wore urban clothing. I was sitting amongst the most powerful gangsters in New Orleans and not one of them was black. After I peeped the scene I wondered would I be right behind Uriah as next to die. A white man who I saw on the news plenty of times, but couldn't put a name with his face spoke first. "Uriah had a feeling his death was soon to be an option when he got into a territory war with the other boss of the black community. So you have an opportunity to take over both of their territories since both of them eliminated themselves. I know it's a lot for you to take in with your mentor being gone, but every guy you see sitting here in this vehicle will now take on Uriah's role as your mentors. His passing was a blessing in disguise for you. Get back to me by next Friday. In the meantime this will be your point of contact (he hands me a card) if you need a murder, a drug, or enforcement." I said thank you in a respectful manner and exited the vehicle. I used my grief as a shield to hide my reaction to the ruthlessness they showed by clearing out Uriah's position without any compassion.

I searched for my ex because I needed her almost as badly as she needed me. I initially got in the game because I was on the verge of getting put out of college due to my lack of payments and I needed money to eat. Now I felt trapped. If there was ever a way out of the game, it just got ten times harder now that the most important shot callers in New Orleans, knew my name, my dirt, and my movements. Bianca was the only person I knew that could relate to my situation but there was no way she wanted me to leave the game. She would probably even want me back if she knew I had cocaine and heroin on deck. It was amazing how my new girl pushed me to stop hustling and my old girl pushed me to keep hustling.

My ex and I only stayed at the repass for a short while. We initially were not supposed to stop at the repass, but we were hungry and wanted the free food. As I sat in the car while she ran inside to grab some wings and bell peppers, I saw Caron standing on the side of the building smoking a cigarette as if it were the last blunt on earth. My ex waived at Caron as if she had to acknowledge him, but didn't want anyone to see. Wow, I could not believe how small the world was and how big Uriah was to the community. My ex's friend bought her car to the repass, so we got in her whip and headed to her house. As soon as I closed her front door after we got inside Bianca pushed me to the ground, and ripped my clothes off as if I had breakaway apparel on, and initiated the best make up sex known to mankind. It was the type of make-up sex to find another problem just so y'all could have it again. Although we had sex for several hours, I had come to the conclusion mid-stroke that I wanted this to be the last time we had sex. I wasn't mad at her for the way she stormed out on me in Biloxi. If anything it was my fault that she stormed out on me like that. I wanted to permanently part ways with Bianca because I concluded that I could not get to where I wanted in life with her as my woman.

After so much time went by I realized that I neglected to tend to Lisa. I had twenty-five missed calls from her and this was the first time I ever missed her call. My ex put her head over my shoulder while I checked my phone and asked, "Was it her?" After she saw the look on my face after I said, "The only her is you. I just need to get up and go take care of some business." Bianca demanded that I stay another thirty minutes as if I did not have an option. I went to the bathroom and texted Hassan where to meet me at in twenty minutes. I told him to come early so he could scope out the scene. "Too cautious" were two words that no drug dealers ever said. Circling the block before parking or meeting with someone was always the norm. The thirty minutes flew by because she fucked my brains out again. As I began to put my clothes back on she tried to stall me again. This time she did not have a reason to, because we had sex more than five times and it was obvious she could not go anymore. I went back to the bathroom to check my phone so I could avoid hearing her mouth. When I got to the bathroom I had eight messages from Hassan. Hassan was parked on the corner at the beginning of the block. He sent a text to alert me that a car of four people were circling the block in drive by mode. When I exited the bathroom my ex suddenly became pushy to get me to leave the house. I took my time to get to the door until I could get Hassan to answer the phone, but his phone went dead. Hassan was the type of friend that if you set a time, you did not have to call him again to confirm it because he would be there. I opened the front door, but left the screen door closed. I grabbed my ex and put her back against the screen door and kissed her passionately to make it look like I was not about to leave anytime soon. When the car that kept circling Bianca's house made a right at the end of the block I jumped off the porch and sprinted to Hassan's car and we peeled off before the other car could make the block again. Hassan disregarded every stop sign for the next mile but somehow the car that was circling my ex's house found us. They trailed us from a distance. It was obvious they were after me. My ex called and asked, "Why did I run out the house and pull off so fast?"

I could not think of who would want to kill me. I was a person who everyone liked and had respect for. As we cruised back to our hood I called Lisa back because I knew she was frantic. She raised her voice at me for the first time. I did not understand her general concern for my safety if she did not know what just happened. After I talked to her for a few minutes it was clear that she had no clue what just happened. Her not hearing from me had her thinking the worse. She began to cry as she told me three of her brothers were killed in the streets and that's why she hated the fact that I hustled. How could I continue to have love for something that the person who I was in love with hated the most? When I arrived home Caron called me and asked where I was. I lied and told him I went out of town because I did not want to be bothered. He asked could I come back in town tomorrow to make the deal happen.

The next morning I figured that it was important to learn more about Derrick's case. When I clicked on the video with Derrick's mugshot the video said, "Derrick Wallace indicted on first degree murder charges of well-known businessman, Uriah Campbell." It all made sense now. The guy who I seen on the news a few times in the back of the van was telling me about this, but I didn't think to put Derrick as Uriah's killer although everything happened simultaneously. The way the media portrayed it Derrick was a savage who was a threat to society and Uriah was an innocent businessman who lived his life as a law abiding citizen. They also used a picture of him in a suit to show who he was and they used one of Derrick's old mugshots from a previous arrest to show who he was. As the district attorney began to brief the media on the case, I saw the same man who offered me the deal to take over the territories behind the district attorney.

After the media painted their picture of who they wanted the bad guy and good guy to be, I decided to paint my own. I felt the gangster who I seen on the news was the worse one out of all of us. His name was Jake. Jake was the type of person that only a mother could love. He was a trust-fund baby who had the ultimate sense of entitlement. He wanted to control the moves made by politicians and the moves made on the street also. Jake came from different walks of life than me and most other drug dealers. Most people sell drugs because their opportunities are limited to make ends meet. Jake was a popular lobbyist and real estate guy in New Orleans. Out of all the gangsters in the van I was the most afraid of him. A man this evil could cover up his crimes with suits and cash. Jake had more ability to cover up his crimes than the average gangster. He wasn't amongst those that were elected officials for the city, but he had as much power as them, and in some cases even more power. People like him made it hard for any city to flourish. My sense of feeling trapped in the game ballooned because the final say in the streets was coming from the top.

The day I was set to meet with Caron felt like a game day for basketball. The only people I talked to on game day were my team. Hassan and I kept in touch throughout the day, but Caron did not pick up the phone once. I knew the deal was going down for sure though. Because of the paranoia that was caused by the car following me I decided to invited my cousin-in-law Shooter. His name said it all. Shooter was a whispered about contract killer from uptown. I was glad that he was available for the mission. Shooter rarely came out of the house. The reason it was so easy to get him to come was because he always felt as if he owed me a favor that he could never repay me for. I threw him on my cousin Keisha when he was a teenager and they had been married for over ten years. I sometimes forgot about Shooter's existence due to his lack of presence. Having him on my team that day made me feel an extra sense of security when I already thought I was untouchable. Every time Shooter had a mission to do he always left the house first thing in the morning because he needed to temporarily detach himself from his family before he executed people. Remembering that Shooter was a loving father and husband, but still a contract killer gave me the reality that I could not put it past Derrick that he wasn't capable of murdering Uriah. Shooter spent the entire day with me. He didn't smoke or drink. If Shooter was around it he had to have food. I was always known as a master chef in the hood. I cooked almost every day after Hurricane Katrina when I moved back to New Orleans. I had a house by myself since fifteen years old and groceries were in abundance because of the Hurricane devastation perks. Almost everybody who came to my house had tasted my food. This was our first time hanging together since Katrina so I decided to lace him up with a meal before we went to the backyard so I could smoke. Even though Shooter rarely left the house, he still knew what went on in the streets before it actually went down. I could not wait to ask him if he knew Derrick and Uriah.

I decided to introduce each situation independently. When I asked Shooter did he know Uriah he stood up and asked how well did I know him with a voice full of suspicion. I decided to tell him how. It made no sense to hide it at that point. Before I could even tell him how I knew Uriah, Shooter got super emotional and said, "I use to work for that nigga. They did him dirty. I could not even make it to the funeral. Uriah had linked with this new cat in town. Those two joined forces and tried to take over the city. Uriah and this white collar gangster were cool until Uriah started doing business with the new cat. White collar wanted Uriah to kill the new cat since he felt the new guy stepped on his toes and his money started slowing down. Uriah refused to kill him, so white collar had a young boy kill Uriah. White collar played him like a drum. The young boy had got on with Uriah and the new cat. I told both of them not to fuck with him, but they ain't listen. One day the young boy was riding with the new cat and stole his wallet out of the middle console, then killed Uriah later that same night. After young boy killed Uriah he left the new cat's wallet at the crime scene to frame him. White collar just did not want two black dudes holding that much power in the city. White collar wants the new reckless young boy who killed Uriah to take over the city. I am thinking about moving to another city to put in work because I would have to kill that little boy." After Shooter finished running it to me about Uriah I asked him did he know Derrick. He responded "That was the new cat who they set up! Derrick had just moved in from Harlem, and got things popping real quick. The white man could not stand him. Derrick was loved in the city and amongst the other kingpins. Fuck I even loved him. He was the only person who I did hits for besides Uriah since I started working for people. He had a great heart. He didn't even want me working for him." Shooter responded.

Caron finally called me on time to ensure that I was ready to make the deal. Hassan rode with me and Shooter trailed five blocks behind us so he could follow the people that followed me. I did not want Caron to be a part of what was following me. My hope was that Shooter could address the people who were previously following me at Bianca's house if they followed me this time. We rode to the deal in silence. I wanted my undivided attention on everyone who got behind us. My gun was on my lap the entire ride until we got to the other side of town. We got to the area twenty minutes before the scheduled time to scope out everything. No car followed us there. I called Caron ten minutes later. No answer. I called a second time closer to the time. He answered in a rushed manner and said, "I am on the way there from the hospital boss man. Park and wait for me across from the po-boy shop." I parked a block back. Shooter parked three blocks back. After five minutes of waiting he decided to circle the perimeter of the neighborhood. He did not believe in sitting still parked but he wanted us to sit still so he could see if we were being followed. I became irritated because Caron was still nowhere in sight. I called him again and he said he was almost there. I decided to get the duffle bag out of the trunk so I could be ready for the transaction. When I got to the trunk a homeless guy with three teeth said, "Hey big man. Could you spare some money?" Most homeless people in New Orleans are relentless as the witnesses of Jehovah. I told him no twice but he kept on pleading his case. I got back in the car to call

Shooter to let him know the guy I was meeting up with was almost here. I decided to get back out the car and apologize to the homeless guy. Before I could get all of the way out of the car Shooter called back and said, "It was a hit. Get ready."

This was the beginning of the blurry part of my night. Caron called me and told me to meet Reggie at the end of the corner by the po-boy spot. He was two blocks ahead of me so I had a play. I asked the homeless man how much money did he want. He responded $7.79. I got excited because he made it evident that he was desperate for money. I put my hand on his shoulder and told him, "I got more for you if you do this favor for me." I emptied the duffle bag on the passenger's seat floor then showed him a bag of cocaine and said, "I will give you a bag of coke if you deliver this duffle bag up the corner for me." The homeless man's face lit up and he said, "I will clean your car with a paper towel for that bag of coke. Give me that duffle bag youngblood." He tried to take off to make the transaction before I gave him instructions. I stopped him and gave him my hat and my shirt to put on and told him to pull his brim real low and exchange bags with the person on the corner. He replied, "I used to do this before you were born big man. I was moving work back when black people weren't even allowed to walk on this street we standing on right now." Reggie only saw me twice, and he wasn't the attentive type to remember my face if he saw me. The rockhead glided up the street so smoothly. It was an entirely different pace from when he first approached me. When he first approached me it looked like he was walking on hot coals. The po-boy shop was on a two way street. I sent the rockhead up the street about ten seconds before I decided to pull off to park across from the po-boy spot. By the time we parked it had looked as if I got out of the car when the rockhead passed our car. A guy that did not look like Reggie with a hood on approached the corner where the transaction was supposed to be made. It was Caron! As soon as I saw that it was Caron, Shooter flew up the street rapidly. Caron and Shooter both neared the rockhead at the same time. Caron pulled a gun out his waist

56

before he could even tell it wasn't me. Caron was dropped by a flurry of bullets from Shooter before he could get one shot off. Caron laid lifeless on the ground. His phone fell out of his pants when he hit the ground. I ran to grab his phone and to look my supposed killer in his face for the last time as he took his last few breaths. He died with his eyes open. Everyone in the streets knew people who died with their eyes open had been dealt karma from taking others' lives.

Before I could get back in the car Shooter peeled off to follow the car that pulled off as soon as Caron got laid flat. As we followed Shooter I read through Caron's text messages on a rocket scientist reading level. Everything was in one place for me. It was a burner phone. There were only texts from a group message with Jake and the other bosses, a group text with Tyrone and Reggie, plus messages from an unsaved number that looked familiar. I searched the # in my phone and it was my ex's number. Bianca had set me up, and the waitress from the restaurant when I first met Uriah was the getaway driver. Uriah had planned on grooming me to be next up. Caron initially had a forty year sentence but he got it reduced because he killed three people in jail for Jake. Bianca was fucking Jake and Caron. Jake was married with five kids and Caron was her ex-boyfriend that never went anywhere but absent in the public eye. Caron was absent from Bianca in the public eye but he was present in her bedroom. Jake and Caron were cool with that. It made them even closer because Jake felt prideful about fucking a young black thug's ex-girlfriend and Caron felt prideful because he was fucking a rich white man's mistress. I wasn't the only person who she set up. She set up her Uncle Uriah also. How could this bitch? Uriah tried to keep his niece out the street because he hated what the game came with. She rode with Caron because she loved everything that the game came with and would let nothing get in the way of what she loved, nothing. I was supposed to be a casualty of war because Uriah wanted me to be heir to the throne because he sensed his death was near. I was the only person standing in the way of Caron.

57

Jake knew Caron was too reckless to run the city, and it would be a suicide mission. After the suicide and homicide missions would have been complete Jake would have been behind several murders without getting his hands dirty.

We lost Shooter. He had been chasing the car too fast. Hassan and I did not say a word on the way home. I went the next three days without speaking to anyone. On the fourth day I decided to reach out to Shooter and Hassan. Shooter's phone was dead and Hassan was nowhere to be found. I went to the park to hang out and ear hustle on what had been going on in the streets. It was quiet and dead in the park at five in the evening like it was five in the morning. I gave the park a little life when I walked through. I asked why everyone was down. A little kid said Shooter got shot up. It was mind-blowing that Shooter never left the house but he was a household name in the streets even to young kids. I knew which hospital he was at because Shooter had no insurance. Word had got out about Caron also. It was no surprise to anyone that he got killed. He had an expiration date with the way he moved around in the streets. I pretended I left the park for another reason and made my way to the hospital.

When I got to Shooter's room he had just flat lined. Hassan was on the floor crying. Hassan looked at me with a face full of tears and wolfed, "He is not going to make it." Shooter had cornered in the car he followed after he killed Caron and killed two people in the getaway car but the survivor shot him several times before he could leave the scene. A once in a lifetime football prospect that was an assumed lock to go to the pros had flat lined at the age of twenty nine in the hospital from gunshot wounds. Shooter blamed his best friend for his demise in life. During Shooter's junior year in high school his best friend jumped on his back after Shooter scored a touchdown. Shooter then awkwardly fell and tore his ACL. Unlike what Shooter thought, I knew the real reason for his demise. The defective public school system was the main cause for his downfall in life. Shooter was always given

58

preferential treatment in school because of his football status. Shooter disregarded the special treatment and went as hard in the classroom as he did on the football field. He was actually a nerd, but it was never acknowledged because of his giant stature and physical talent. Test taking was a flaw of his but he counteracted it by studying excessively. If he was not extra prepared for anything, he panicked. The private school I attended prepared their students for the ACT and SAT in middle school. The public high school Shooter and I attended did not prepare students for those standardized tests until their senior year. Many people wrongfully assume that standardized tests are an accurate assessment of a student's intelligence. Shooter's last step before getting accepted to college was the ACT test. College coaches began pressuring Shooter to take the test the summer after his eleventh grade year. Prior to that Shooter did not know anything about the ACT. The coaches were appalled and began to show concern about the education he received. Their astonishment gave Shooter severe anxiety about taking the ACT test. He felt it was too late to prepare accordingly. Shooter scored a 13 on the first and only time he took the test. I think you get 12 points for writing your name. The stigma of being a dumb athlete was something Shooter profusely worked to avoid his entire athletic career. After word got out about his ACT score he was labeled as a dumb athlete in the media, on the internet, and almost everywhere he went in life. The fact that he would not be able to play football his senior year and the scrutiny of his test scores convinced Shooter to drop out of high school the second week of football season. His lack of guidance was the cherry on top of his demise. Junior colleges would have accepted Shooter and his poor test score, but there weren't any junior colleges that had a football team in Louisiana. Not only did that mean there were less opportunities for high school students in Louisiana who wanted to continue their academic and athletic career at the same time, it meant most people in Louisiana were uneducated on the Junior College route. Everyone in the state thought his talents were too great to take to a junior college. People who thought that were sadly mistaken because some of the best professional football players played at Junior Colleges. With that being said Shooter felt he was too good for Junior college. After he dropped out of high school his first job was working at a fast-food restaurant. That did not last long. He got fired before he could receive his first paycheck. A customer cursed Shooter out because the ice cream machine was broke. Shooter broke the customers jaw, and shoulder with one punch. After the fast-food restaurant he tried telemarketing but so many people recognized his unique voice. Everyday people would remind him of what he should have been athletically and he couldn't handle it. Because his dreams in life were ended, he didn't mind if he ended other's lives.

I always looked at the "crabs in a barrel" term differently when referring to the black community. That phrase needs to be depicted deeper. People focus more on the crabs than the barrel. Black people were placed in the barrel simultaneously when we were placed in the United States for slavery. The barrel is the porous conditions that have transcended from slavery to current day ghettos and economic structures which are designed to put the black race in a state of genocide. Black people have been continuously born into that barrel for centuries. Some crabs made it out, but most of those crabs are so quick to run from the barrel that they don't concern themselves to go back to show the remaining crabs how to make it out. Energy would be more efficiently exerted trying to change the structure of the barrel rather than on another crab. It is so easy for one crab to step on another crab in the barrel because of the close proximity and barely anybody in the barrel knows the correct way to make it out. Shooter is just one example of a crab in the barrel. He was not born a killer, and had much more to offer in life besides running a football. Shooter felt he only had one way to make it out and lost his mind after that one way was destroyed. That motivated him to destroy the other crabs in the barrel.

We followed Shooter as they rolled his body to the morgue then disbursed after that. When Shooter died I felt he left the wrong part of him with me when he passed. The walk to the car was accompanied with a face full of cold tears that chilled my cheeks as they fell to the ground. When I opened my car door I felt two small fists on my back and a weak push. I used that momentum to reach in the glovebox to grab my gun. After I opened the glove compartment I heard Lisa's voice cursing at me. I had really lost my mind. I almost pulled a gun on my girlfriend because I was so paranoid from everything I was going through. It took for me to see Lisa to register that I had not reached out to her over the past several days. We got in the backseat as the sun went down and I laid in her arms. I did not know where to start. When I opened my mouth I cried tears out until I got thirsty. I had too much to say and too much pain to put it into words. When I opened my eyes the windows in my car were cracked, my shirt was off, the sun was up, and I had the imprint of my girl's jeans on my face. I had slept the night away in her arms. Before I could thank her for getting me through the night she exited the backseat and said, "Let me know when you are done with the streets so you could start back with me."

That morning was the first one I spent at home since the day Caron was killed. I had been spending nights away from the house to stay low in case Shooter's killer wanted retaliation. The next morning Hassan was on the porch waiting for me. Instead of having a durag and shorts on, he had his old work uniform on. Hassan's lease was almost up and he decided it was time to transition not only from his current house, but his current lifestyle. He didn't have to say a word for me to know he was done with the streets. We did not even have a formal discussion about him leaving the game, but it was obvious he was finished.

Chapter 7

I was officially alone in the game after Hassan moved the work back out of his trunk into mines. I decided to move the drugs into the house for the first time so I did not have to ride around with it. My dad had some of his belongings there but rarely came over so I wrapped the drugs in a pillow case and put them under the nightstand in my bedroom. The only place I wanted to be right now was with my girl. Lisa picked me up after Hassan left for work and told me she wanted to take me somewhere. This was the second time a woman had ever taken me anywhere and to my surprise it was a bookstore. When we arrived there we had coffee and she took me to the back of the bookstore which was the kids section. After we sat down she leaned towards me and asked, "What happened those days you were gone?" I told her every single thing, from start to finish, and didn't miss a detail. I talked for over an hour and she listened to me with her undivided attention. At the end of the story she didn't say anything for about thirty seconds then said, "Look around at this area. Do you want to be alive to take your kids here? Are you interested to see what life has to offer you besides selling drugs and an early coffin? Stay here and think about it." She walked off and left me lying on the colorful beanbags for several hours. I did not wonder where she was going and what time she would come back.

After the sun went down I realized I wanted kids, and God had sent me a woman who I wanted to give one to. My experiences were rare in life. I was able to see both sides of the spectrum. The richest of the rich and the poorest of the poor. Falling victim to the hood is falling victim to oppression. One of my favorite things about the United States is that while you may be born into poverty, you could grow to be rich if you play your cards right. Many people in other countries are entrapped in poverty forever and have no options to make it out.

Lisa finally picked me up from the bookstore around 7:00pm. As we rode home I pleaded to her that I was done with the game and elaborated on what the bookstore did for me. I felt I was reborn again. She said, "That's great, but I am dropping your ass off at home tonight. You need to spend a little more time thinking about how stupid you felt sleeping with a girl who tried to kill you." She got me. I had forgotten all about bringing up that I slept with my ex because she didn't react when I told her at the library. As we got to my house I saw my dad turning off the street with his old bed on the back of his truck. I hadn't seen my dad in forever. I couldn't believe how long it had been since we sat down and had a real conversation. My girl continued to show her pettiness by pulling off fast as soon as I closed her passenger door.

My life began to feel a tad bit normal again. I had a legitimate game plan to make it out and the dust had almost settled in the drug game. When I walked through the house, I saw so many of my dad's belongings. It was safe to say that he moved back home. I had been through so much that my dad didn't know who I was anymore or where I was at in life. My first stop when I got home was the kitchen. I had not read my mail in forever and there were piles of it on the counter. Almost all of my mail had been opened. I rarely received any mail besides birthday letters and basketball recruiting letters. My days of getting recruited for basketball were over and my birthday was not anytime soon so I was curious to see where all the mail had come from. I almost forgot I opened a new bank account. All of my statements were opened from my initial $50 deposit to the most recent monthly statement. I could not do anything but smile after being able to see how far I came financially on paper. I parlayed to my room with the biggest smile on my face to save my account statements for memorabilia. I heard the alarm on the front door go off, but I knew that was my dad. As I searched through the nightstand, my dad walked close behind me and asked, "Is this what you are looking for?" Before I could respond my dad put all of his three hundred pounds into three punches that connected perfectly with my face. When I hit the ground he threw my bag of drugs at me and barked, "Get the fuck out, you got fifteen seconds!" I put three pairs of underwear in my bag then dashed out of the house.

When I realized I left my keys inside there was no way in hell I was going back inside to get them. Not only did I leave my keys, I left plenty of other essentials. Most importantly my wallet, keys, and phone charger. I took my phone but only had 5% even though I had a charger with me the entire day. Figuring out how to use that 5% was a struggle. Involving my girl in what just happened was not an option. That would have been the nail in the coffin of our relationship if she knew I was selling heroin and cocaine. Hassan had not moved into his new place yet and going next door by him was not an option. I was tripping with no map. There was nowhere for me to go. The streetcar line was only two miles away from my house. As I walked to the streetcar I did not know which direction I would go geographically or in life. The only identification I had in my possession was my student ID. I could not get a hotel with that. After I got on the streetcar I sat next to a homeless person. It finally hit me that I would be living as he was for the time being. I picked his brain the entire ride about how he got by then exited the streetcar when I got near my university. My finals were seven days away. My graduation was dependent on me scoring over a B on all of my exams. Test taking was never a strength of mines but I had to turn it into one. Passing those finals were the only way I could make it out of the streets. For the week leading up to finals I studied at 6:00am until midnight on campus. During my hours of studying I found a place around campus to safely hide my narcotics. When all of the facilities were shut down I found different places to sleep outside every night. Passing my finals had me so locked in that I did not realize I was homeless until my first exam. Scoring over a B or above was the only thing that mattered.

Even if I had a roof to lay my head under during that timeframe I would have barely utilized it because I was always in the library.

After getting a whiff of how I smelled when I sat down for my first exam I could not go another day homeless. I smelled like hand soap, paper towels, and weed. When I crossed the threshold of my first exam I dialed Hassan's phone number immediately to see if he moved into his new place yet. There could not have been a less ideal time in life to be living by Hassan. He usually had over ten guests in his apartment all day. The people were not a threat to me but his guests could not keep it down while they played video games in his one bedroom apartment. However Hassan could not have been a better host. He let me sleep in his room during my entire stay and also made a copy of his house key for me. My only responsibility was to cook and cooking was an outlet for me. Hassan had proved I could trust him forever for the fifteenth time in life. He did not touch a gram of the drugs that I left unattended in his possession. Hassan also did me the ultimate favor of gathering my things from my father's house. He and my girl helped move my things without me because my dad was not ready to see my face again. That time period made me realize true requirements for a friendship. If you can trust someone with your money, your spouse, your family and how they treat you behind your back then they are a true friend. If someone could only be trusted with three of those four things then they are not your true friend.

College was almost behind me, but I had no idea what was in front of me. Church was my second safe haven after basketball growing up, but I stopped going to church because my views on religion was changed drastically during my sophomore year in college. That year I enrolled in an African American history class. Caucasians were the main focus of every history class I took until then. According to the history classes offered by primary and secondary schools in the United States students are given the impression that

Caucasians were the only reasons for the country's economic success. If a student did no research outside of the classroom they would be led astray to believe that black people only had minimal contributions to the history of the United States. Black people are notoriously depicted as slaves in the United States history courses. A countless number of slave-owners are considered heroes of U.S history. Slavery still has an impact on the black American community economically, mentally, and financially. No amount of reparations would be fair compensation for centuries of oppression. Only a meniscal amount of black Americans of the African descent are highlighted in history books. Even most African American museums or documentaries produced in the U.S only speak about a small amount of black Americans who preceded us in history. Those iconic black figures are recycled amongst most studies of black Americans. Therefore I starved for knowledge of black American history. When I enrolled in my first African-American history class I finally got a taste of what I had been looking for. My people who I thirsted to learn more about were now the main subject of study. This area of study was not mandatory growing up and it was not even offered as an elective to me. My knowledge about my roots was nugatory.

One life changing lesson that I learned was that Africans were not practicing the catholic religion before they were delivered to the United States. The catholic religion was presented to my ancestors to have them under strict uniform mind control, to focus them on the afterlife instead of enjoying life on earth, and to make them forgiving of their masters who held them captive while they tortured the men and raped the women. The depictions of the two most popular figures in the catholic religion, a white Jesus and a white Santa Clause plays a large underlying factor in the mindset of black Americans who feel inferior to white people. If those two figures are praised growing up, odds of seeing the white man as supreme skyrockets. White figures exclusively dominate not only U.S history, but the catholic religion also. After furthering my education about the catholic religion I abruptly cut my ties. I began to mix my own logic along with my unfiltered personal belief about everything the Catholic religion presented to me. I did not agree with many things that I unconsciously followed growing up i.e. there was no way I could believe that killing a man and premarital sex were equivalent in sin. As a child my mind was so gone that I believed I would die in my sleep if I did not say my prayers right. After I freed myself from the catholic religion I was able to have a closer relationship with God. Even though I was done with the Catholic religion there were still a few things I liked about church. I had an affinity for being around people praising a higher power and confession.

Confession was exactly what I needed at the time. Confession it was. I decided to go to confession at the Mega-church where Uriah's funeral was. I took my girl's car to remain low-key. Reverend Wilson had recently built a Mega-church in Mid-City. Rev. was a former crack dealer from uptown. He found God in prison. He was one of the few success stories in the streets, but his respect had diminished after word got out that he testified against his best friend for a reduced sentence. He was initially offered a deal for a thirty year prison sentence, but his sentence was lowered down to five years with good time after he allegedly ratted on his best friend. He was released from prison the same year I finished high school and now he already appeared to be a millionaire. As a kid I loved confession because I felt free after I was able to vent about my sins without repercussions.

When I arrived at the Mega-church it felt like I pulled up at a prestigious business or social event. The church offered valet service, reserved parking, and had foreign cars outside of the church. It seemed so out of place in the hood. The Mega-church was in a five mile radius of three public housing developments. When I got out of the car I spotted a few of my elders heading towards confession also so I let them go in first. As I walked back to my car I heard a voice I hadn't heard in ages. An extremely raspy voice yelled, "What's up?" to me. Before I could turn my head I already knew who it was. It was

Peanut. I had not seen Peanut since he dropped out in 9th grade. All you had to do was look in Peanut's face to realize that he had a past. Peanut was one of the grimiest gangsters in New Orleans. He specialized in armed robberies and caught two murder cases but beat both. Being that Peanut beat two murder cases before he was eighteen years old and was arrested over twenty times he was on his last straw with the judicial system. Peanut and I were friends to the extent that we could go several years without speaking to each other and pick up where we left off. Waiting for confession was a perfect time for us to do just that.

We decided to hotbox my car before we went to confession. After Peanut inhaled his first puff he began to tell me about several murders that he committed and that he did armed robberies on a weekly basis. His little brother getting killed as retaliation for a murder he committed made him want to give the streets up for good. We were at confession for the same reason. We wanted to hand our past lives to the Lord and move on from the streets. Peanut told me that he came to confession the past three weeks but just sat outside because he did not have the courage to go in. "I am glad that you came to confession today my brother, this is my sign that it is time for me to go in", Peanut said. We put the blunt out and made our way to the confessional area.

I decided to go first because I knew Peanut would be a while with all the sins he had to confess. Before I went into the booth I told Peanut I would wait for him in the car after he finished so I could take him home. For the first few minutes I was in the confession booth I could not utter a word. "Are we here to meditate?" asked Reverend Wilson. I could not believe it was him. I felt comfortable when he spoke because he had experienced the streets before. I vented almost everything that happened over the past two years. After I finished venting he responded, "You are at a point in your life when you are about to accomplish something major that will transition you onto bigger and better things." My problems and sins felt like they were left in the booth. I hugged Peanut when I left out and told him, "Let it all out, I will be in the car waiting for you."

I sparked back up when I got in my car and put on some gospel music. Peanut was in there for almost an hour. No other cars had pulled up while I sat there and waited. As soon as Peanut exited the church a flock of police cars burst into the parking lot and jumped the curve to corner him in. Peanut surrendered and they arrested him. He looked up to the sky and cursed his heart out. I was scared to make a move because I did not know if I was next to get arrested. I stayed in my car until the scene cleared out. As I cranked my car up I saw Reverend Wilson walk out the side of the church. I had a good enough view to see him but he could not see me. I was a deer in headlights when I saw him because I did not know if I should approach him about what just happened or avoid him. During the stage of contemplation a black van creeped into the parking lot. It was the same van that I sat in with the kingpins after Uriah's funeral. The van pulled up where Rev. was waiting in isolation while smoking a cigarette. After the van was in park for ten seconds Jake exited the passenger's side. Jake handed pastor an envelope stuffed with money, and a pat on the back. After Jake vacated the premises Rev. took a seat on the bench and smoked a cigarette harder than anyone whoever laid lips on a cigarette. After he tossed the butt of the cigarette he sunk his head in his hands.

Pastor had sold out Peanut to Jake for financial gain. He had also sold out the community right along with most Mega-Churches in the United States. Mega-Churches are given grants by the government, receive north of $12,000,000 every Sunday from collections, and still have not provided any economic change for the community it exploits. With all of the money that has been put into these Mega churches there is nothing to show for what the church has done for the black community economically. The Mega-Church has not erected any hospitals, universities, or jobs that could provide economic change in the black community. The black community in the United States does not hold the Mega-church economically responsible for anything.

After I left from the church I decided to go hang out at the park in my hood to ease my mind. The playground was the environment that was most comfortable to me. I was loved in the park. Respect in the hood is one of the most prized possessions anyone can have from there. It can't be purchased, and it's hard to obtain. I previously refrained from smoking in the park because the first time I smoked there people aggravatingly bought up my basketball career, but I did not give a half of a fuck about that anymore. Life slowed down with every puff I took and I noticed things I never seen before. My inner circle at the park consisted of five men. Two were always in and out of jail, two of them had not finished high school, and the other one had no ambition in life. I understood everyone had different paths in life but none of those guys were on similar paths as me. These were people who I turned to for advice and confirmation on ideas. How could they tell me if I was wrong? How could they build upon a business idea? How could they help my future? They could not.

My phone rang and it was my academic advisor. I walked off because I had to pretend to be sober without making my friends laugh at me. My academic advisor said, "You will be a part of the graduating class of 2012 congratulations!" I thanked her and ran back to the basketball court to tell my friends the great news. "What happened? What happened?" they yelled as they began celebrating. When I responded, "I am graduating", I was the only person still celebrating. My accomplishment was not good news to them and they did not understand the significance. It's crazy how your circle of friends change as what you are doing in life changes. The prior year I hung with college and professional athletes because I was a college athlete. The following year I hang with killers and drug dealers because I was a drug dealer. I did not know exactly what I wanted to be at that moment, but I knew the people that I was hanging with could not help me get there.

I was never that confident about taking exams but I knew I passed all of my finals because of how prepared I was. In eighteen years of schooling I never got straight A's on any exams. It proved that anything is possible when you go all out for it. Because I previously never accomplished that in such a lengthy time span I deemed it to be impossible. Your hard work can make anything possible no matter how impossible the task at hand may appear. I did not know if I would graduate before the phone call from my academic advisor so consequently I did not mail out any invitations for my tentative graduation date. Normally during times when you accomplish major feats such as a college graduation they are to be celebrated to its extremity but I could not because I still had the conundrums of figuring out what to do with the drugs and what to do after I crossed the stage.

During the week prior to graduation I decided to spend as much time with my girl as possible and also reconcile everything with my dad. Whichever transition I was going to make in life after graduation I had to make sure I had them by my side. My dad was reluctant to meet up with me, but he changed his mind once I admitted I was wrong for what I did and expressed my regret for it. I was not only nervous about what I was going to do after graduation; I was worried about living to see graduation also. I still had drugs to sell, Shooter's killer was still on the loose, and so was my ex-girlfriend who tried to set me up. Time changes when you are living in a state of paranoia. Every second is a day, every minute is a week, and every week is a year when you are paranoid.

Jude, a friend I met in college decided to throw me a graduation party. The turnout for my party was amazing. People from my elementary school, my hood, my college, and people who had love for me throughout the city was there. I could not believe that many people had love for me. So many people could not believe that I was still able to graduate from a top ranked college after all of the hardships and experiences I had endured along my journey. It was even hard for me to believe it. I wondered why no one showed me love like this on a consistent basis. Life baffles you when people come out the woodworks to show love for you after you accomplish something major or after you pass along. All I could do was smile because of everyone's presence which I appreciated so much. I had no clue these people still had love for me because I had not spoken to some of them in years. I wanted to give them something else to celebrate. I would have hated to look down from heaven and see all those people celebrating my passing without seeing that night. If it weren't for the graduation party I would have been surprised to see more than half of these people at my funeral. I got so drunk that night my brother and a friend had to carry me out the club. On the way to my hotel I just prayed that I would make it to see the sunrise. Lisa drove me back to my hotel room as I continued to throw up in my lap. I was not even worried about graduation the next morning because I figured I would be too hungover to make it anyway.

Thankfully I woke up at 6:00am with no alarm clock the next morning. My graduation day had come. It was evident that nothing could stop me in life. A hurricane, a life of poverty, my ex trying to kill me, a hangover, nothing! I cleaned up, put my cap and gown on, and then headed to the Superdome for my graduation. My college graduation was the first time I graduated from a predominately white school so I did not know what to expect at the graduation. Graduates had on pajamas pants, and sweatpants under their gowns. Some graduates even had thong slippers on their feet instead of dress shoes. Also there was a full bar on the floor at graduation. That would have been great if I could stomach the smell of alcohol. I napped the entire graduation until it was almost time to walk across the stage. When I walked across the stage it was one of the most relieving feelings ever. Everything weighing me down was finally off of my back. After a day of celebrating with my family and friends I decided to go back to the hotel room. I was too burnt out to do anything else that night. When I woke up the next morning I sat and looked out the window onto the view of the city skyline and I knew it was time to move on.

I called my family from Houston, Texas that came to celebrate my graduation to let them know I would be following them back to Houston. I did not know what I would tell my dad or my girl, but I would rather be alive to tell them than not be. Breaking the news of my plans to relocate was the last thing I wanted to do, but they deserved to hear it from me rather than someone else. My dad and Lisa took it way better than I expected. They knew it was best for me to move away so I could change my life. My family wanted to leave at noon so I decided to parlay around the city to fully take in the last hours of living in the city that scarred me so deeply.

If I were to move on mentally along with physically then I had to go back to the place that haunted my mind the most. The place that was immovable from my mind was where Caron tried to kill me. It didn't register that I was set up twice until I parked my car when I arrived at my destination. I prayed I would never see my ex and those people who plotted on me again. Only God knows what I would do to them. After standing outside of my car for twenty minutes and I saw a homeless guy walking up the street. I dropped my head and instantly thought about how I put that crackhead who I sent to make the drug transaction in harm's way. Who was I to put an innocent man's life at risk? When I lifted my head back up I realized it was him walking up the street. He walked aggressively towards me and said, "I almost got fucking shot because of you muthafucka! What the fuck you got to say for that?" I could not say anything. I remembered I promised him one thing. I decided to give him the whole duffle bag of drugs instead of one bag. I got the bag out of the trunk and tossed it to him. When I looked at him his eyes watered then I pulled off without saying anything. One might think I was dumb for giving away that much money, but it still wasn't enough to repay a man for risking his life for mines. I felt less guilt for the way I paid my tuition because that is a common legal business practice throughout the country. Resisting to sell what I found in Uriah's trunk also lowered my guilt.

My trials and tribulation growing up made it seem impossible to make it out of the hood. It was discouraging seeing grown people in the hood. Almost everyone there wanted to make it out but could not prevail. The sense of urgency intensified as I got older but so did my doubt. Many people that came before me who I felt were more talented and smarter than me did not make it out. That did not give me much encouragement for the future as a child. Being able to outsmart students who were rich with all of the resources in the world and prevailing from every detrimental situation forced me to develop a level of confidence that some would deem irrational. My untapped potential maximized when I found a love for life and thought about reproducing. I would never be able to lay in my bed at night if my children experienced the same things I did as a child. When I got on I-10 to head to Houston I came to the conclusion that nothing could be harder than to make it out of the streets and that this was my biggest accomplishment in life. I finally made it out. In the streets, I experienced two murders before my eleventh birthday; almost got killed by my ex-girlfriend twice; and an associate tried to murder me. What could be worse than the streets?

Chapter 8

This was the first time I looked into my rearview mirror and did not see any vehicles behind me. All I saw was guns, betrayal, death, and jail behind me. When I looked into the windshield I saw a blank slate. I was being reborn again. Once you start over you have to know that new levels will bring you new devils. I felt there was no way pain in corporate America could compare to pain in the streets. I felt a natural high for four hours en route to Houston and it was blew after I saw red and blue lights in my rearview signaling me to pull over. A police car had been riding behind me for the past three miles looking into my car. I got all my papers switched over to me and was completely legal but every black man in the United States heart drops to his feet after he is pulled over by a police car regardless of his innocence. The goofy looking police officer had a chili bowl haircut and looked like the stereotypical racist cop. The police officer poked his head in my car and asked, "Where are you going boy?" A white man calling a grown black man, "boy" is equivalent to calling him a nigger. I stared in the officer's sunglasses and responded, "Texas". The police asked, "For what?" as if I responded that I was on the way to his mother's house. I responded, "I just graduated from college so I am moving to Texas." "Really? You just walked across someone's stage? What did you get your degree in?" the police officer asked in an astonished manner. I answered "Sociology "and the police began to laugh hysterically and said, "Your degree is useless. You can continue on with your journey headed nowhere. You are free to go."

I spent five years busting my ass through adversity and my degree was not respected amongst my friends and I just got shitted on by a police officer. Was I the only person who knew what my college degree was worth? I still felt unbothered. I decided to spend that summer in Houston partying and living at my brother's house. I was a young black man with a college degree from a top ranked university in the country so I figured that would guarantee me a high paying job when I was ready to start working. It took four months for me to land a gig, and it was an hourly job that barely paid above minimum wage at a popular oil and gas company. My first day in Corporate America was the opposite of what I had dreamed of. Orientation was an insult to my intelligence and my manager's reading level was the level of a struggling middle school student. He struggled severely with his subject verb

75

conjugations. Every sentence was tough on my ears. Come to find out, my manager did not make it pass the 10th grade in high school, but somehow he wound up managing me. I did not have any spite towards him, but he immediately showed spite towards me. After orientation was dismissed he pulled me to the side and said, "Don't show off or show me up, and make sure you always remember who the boss is around here."

During my first lunch break in Corporate America I had no one to sit with. That never happened from my lunch breaks in elementary school up until college. I always had someone to sit with if I wanted to. When I sat down to eat lunch in the cafeteria people from almost every table looked at me as if I did not belong in the same cafeteria as them. That scenario was very reminiscent of my middle school years. I could not even pay someone to sit with me. I opened my phone and decided I would get back on social media for good. While I was walking back to clock in for lunch I uploaded a picture of the company logo that I was working for and a picture of the campus. It was action time after I finished lunch. I was in charge of delivering mail on the second and third floor of the building. Most employees who were on the second floor were lawyers, engineers and other people who held prestigious positions. I was instructed to leave the mail for everyone on the second floor in their mailbox. The employees on the third floor were mainly newcomers and administrative staff. My work area was in the basement of the building. I was so happy to finally be out of the basement since I had to work there the entire morning. My mail runs on the second floor were a breeze. Three people stepped out of there office to introduce themselves as I delivered the mail. When I got to the third floor I knew that was my opportunity to build some rapport and establish relationships. Every employee on the third floor had their name on their office door. When I made it to the first office I walked in and said, "Hello Ms. Schultz." She cut her eyes at me and asked, "How do you know my name? Better yet just leave my mail on my desk." I guess she was not observant enough to notice that her name was on her office door. I figured it may have been a race thing. The next lady's name was Brenda. I knew she was black so I walked in with all the confidence in the world and said, "Heyyy Ms. Brenda." She cut her eyes even harder than Ms. Schultz then rolled her neck and asked, "What you want? Oh you the new mail boy? Don't come in here with all of that, move along." It had to be a class thing. Because they were insecure about their position with the company they wanted to belittle someone who had a lesser position than them. It is amazing how people treat others who they assume can't help them. I went to the bathroom to check my phone and get my pride back together. My pride took a bigger hit when I saw so many people comment on my last post saying how proud they were of me. The status of my new job was a big allusion on social media. The company was elite, but my position was not. My boss had eight years less education than me, and I was disrespected by my colleagues because they felt they were better than me. Maybe the officer who pulled me over was right.

Things became desperate for me. I stopped going out. Celebration time was over. After my first day at the oil and gas company I applied to fifty jobs a day online. During the next month I only got one job interview. My interview with the hiring company was conducted by an employee who had the same position I was interviewing for. He started three days before my interview. To make things even worse, the interview was held at a fast-food restaurant. I excused myself to go to the restroom during the interview and never went back. The feeling that my degree was worthless set in after my second month of not being able to find a better job paying much more than minimum wage. I figured the college degree on my résumé would at least get me one good opportunity out of the three hundred and fifty I applied for every week. Each job I wanted told me they were looking for a candidate with experience. What was college for if my degree was irrelevant for an entry level experience? You have to start from somewhere to earn experience, and the place I started at was not valuable experience. My female best friend Kim who was a sophomore in college at the time had just got a mid-senior level position while she was in college. Here I was with a degree and could not even get an entry level position. I reached out to her and asked how she got the position. She told me she fabricated on her résumé so I did the same thing. After four days of having a fabricated résumé I had four requests for interviews. Corporate America was the first place I experienced where lying paid off.

I did not accrue any vacation hours even though I had been with the company for a few months. I had four inquiries for interviews but had to schedule them all in the same day to avoid getting fired for missing work. Only one company said they could interview me within the next two weeks. They were one of the largest hospitals in Houston. The others were a rental car company, and two other companies that I was not interested in interviewing with. The hospital had an urgent need to fill their vacant position of an operations manager. Urgency was the biggest factor into finding my next position so the want was mutual between me and the hospital, but I felt it was too good to be true. If this opportunity was presented to me when I first moved to Houston I would not have been surprised. Being subjected to the position with the oil and gas company gave me little confidence.

I rode to my interview with the hospital in silence. I always rode in silence when I was on the way to accomplish a major task. When I arrived at the hospital I was directed to sit in the break room of the employees I would potentially be managing. The employees were housekeepers and maintenance men. Almost everyone in the break room knew who I was, and embraced me in a warm manner. I began to feel overly anxious for the interview because I was underqualified for the position and I knew the importance of doing great in the interview. There is nothing I would have changed about how the entire process went. After the interview concluded the recruiter gave me a tour of the hospital. On the tour he explained to me that they were trying to fill the position immediately. The guy who previously filled the position had passed away unexpectedly and there was a lack of applicants because the hospital was a forty-five minute drive outside of city limits.

I rode away from the interview still feeling like the position at the hospital was too good to be true therefore I carried on the next day at work like nothing happened. When I arrived to work three of my co-workers were absent. Jeannine, Raheem, and Jane were missing. Pierre was my only other colleague who showed up to work. It was weird that all three of those employees missed work. Each one of them had situations at home that forced them to work every hour available to them. Jeannine was a single mother of three and had no support system. Raheem was the sole provider for his mother who had cancer. Jane had been working with the company for thirty years and could not get a job elsewhere because she did not have a GED. I called Pierre to the hallway because I was nervous about everyone's absence. "Where is everybody?" I asked Pierre. Pierre put his hand on my shoulder and said, "Look kid, I know you are new to Corporate America, but welcome to the real world. Those three people you are looking for got laid off yesterday morning. Two of them drove an hour just to get told they are fired. All three of them needed this job desperately. But that's how it goes young man. They go quicker than they come, and the ones that go are usually the best ones. Don't feel sad for them. Just focus on getting your GED and getting into college so you don't have to be here struggling like me." Pierre was never short on words and he was still talking but I had to cut him off. I cut him off mid-sentence and said, "I have a college degree Pierre." He looked around as if someone called his name but didn't know from which direction then turned back to me and asked, "Well what the fuck are you doing here? You have to get the fuck from out of here. Our boss doesn't even have a high school diploma.

The feeling of paranoia had worked its way back into my life. This situation made me wonder if the time I spent getting my degree was wasted because I was not guaranteed a job that could pay off my loans I used to get my degree. Another week went by at work, but it felt like an entire year. I usually kept my phone on silent at work but I had to keep my phone on loud and vibrate so I would not miss a call from the hospital. I heard my phone ring and immediately ran to the bathroom because I knew it was the hospital calling before I even looked at the caller ID. The hospital called me back to tell me I got the job. After I got back from the bathroom my manager said, "Don't you ever take that long in the bathroom or you are next to be out the door." I wanted to walk off at that moment but I was given that job by referral, so I could not disgrace the person that referred me regardless of how much I hated the job. As happy as I was, I could not take my mind off my three colleagues who just got laid off. How could a corporation who had so much money not be able to afford to keep these employees that busted their asses on minimum wages to keep their job so they could provide for their family? It felt insane that I had to give this company a two week notice after they fired three of my colleagues without a two hour notice.

My final two weeks with the company sped by and were very different than my first few months. Once word got out about my new position at the hospital the same people that previously turned their face up at me had a new found love and respect for me. I don't even know how some people could even muster up enough pride to go from shitting on me to praising me. I had accomplished what they thought I couldn't. No one besides my manager and Pierre at the oil and gas company knew I had a college degree. The main people who were uncomfortable with their job tried to shit on me for doing mines. My manager had finally eased up on me because he knew I was no longer a threat to take his position. What he failed to realize was that I did not want his position. Pierre was the only person who was sincerely sad about me leaving the company. He took me to lunch on my last day. Once we sat down he leaned over the table and said, "Take your time and look around then tell me what you see? I answered, "Everyone has a suit on except us." Pierre responded, "No, you have to be able to analyze deeper than that son. Everyone you see comes from different walks of life than us. They will never see you as one of them even if you all have the same credentials. None of them will want you to outshine them. This will be a world unlike anything you experienced before. Don't let the shaved faces and suits blind you from the fact that they are some of the biggest gangsters. You will be stabbed in the back without a knife and robbed without a weapon. Move carefully. There are no gangs you can join to help protect you, and you will have to learn on your own. The war against you will be played in an entirely different way than what you are accustomed to."

Chapter 9

I rode in complete silence on the way to my first day of work at the hospital. My commute was an hour and fifteen minutes so I had plenty of time to think on the way to work. I let what Pierre told me marinate in my mind, but I did not think much of it because of all of the tough things I survived in the streets. Nothing could be worse than that. The person who conducted all of my interviews was stationed in Dallas, Texas. He conducted two phone interviews and one in-person interview. As soon as I pulled into the parking lot at work I received a text from him. The text message was to inform me that my manager Roger would be there to get me acclimated and train me. I found it sketchy that he never mentioned anything about the person who would be my direct manager. I felt weird about that but I was so excited to finally be in a position of prestige. The break room was the first place I went when I arrived on the premises. That was where everyone who I managed clocked in and where their lockers were. I arrived during transition time. My shift began at 3:00pm and ended at 1:00am. 3:00pm was a transition time. Transition time was when one shift ended and the next one began. The next transition time came at 12:00am when the second shift of maintenance men and housekeepers ended and the third shift began. Going from delivering mail to managing over fifty employees can be quite intimidating.

When I arrived to the break room it was reminiscent of a high school setting. Everyone was isolated in small groups or by themselves. People were sizing each other up, rolling their eyes at each other, and ignoring each other. My youngest employee was thirty four years old. I was hornswoggled to see people of that age act so childish. When everyone noticed that I got the job, the room erupted. Almost every employee congratulated me. The love felt unreal. A middle age white man who had on waterproof slacks, orthopedic loafers, and a company polo walked through the door of the break room and sharply said, "Party over, calm down, calm down, lets focus on what we came here to do. (Puts hand on my shoulder) This is your new manager. He will be taking over for Larry. Don't give this rookie too hard of a time." The positive energy in the room deflated before he finished talking. I assumed he was Roger. We started on a very bad note from him touching me, but I did not acknowledge it. Once the room got silent the guy with the waterproof khakis on proceeded with the daily huddle. At the conclusion of the daily huddle almost everyone approached me again and expressed how happy they were to have me as their manager before they carried on with their daily duties.

I felt a hand on my shoulder again then the guy who led the huddle said, "Hi, I'm Todd. Welcome to my hospital. I'll be in charge of you, so let me show you around." I blanked out for a second because I thought Roger would be my immediate manager and because of Todd's last few statements. As we walked around the hospital Todd told everyone the same thing as if he were a parrot, "Hey this is the new operations manager. He is taking Larry's position since he decided to pass along." Todd's character began to dampen my mood. Our last stop was the CEO's office. The CEO greeted me warmly and asked, "Are you ok?" I immediately perked back up and got into character. We carried on a great conversation for ten minutes until Todd cut me off mid-sentence and said, "Ok smarty-pants it's time to go". He acted similar to the jealous friend that interrupted their friend while they were being pursued. I had to question where Roger was after our last stop. I asked Todd and he responded, "Roger is gone for a week so I will be in charge of you until he gets back and probably after that since he is my boss. Any questions, concerns, or ideas go through me first. It will not be allowed to go over my head, and you see those people celebrating you in the break room. They are your workers. Do not engage in any conversation with them unless it is work related.

My first day felt like a week. The recruiter told me I was supposed to get trained, but Todd told me that the training was irrelevant and I already knew everything I needed to know. Due to my lack of assignments and structure to my day I decided to dedicate my first week to building rapport with my staff. I was never a manager previous to the hospital experience unlike what my résumé said. I figured it had to be similar to being the leader of a sports team. The biggest problem with my staff appeared to be that no one enjoyed coming to work. Coaching was the biggest thing that impacted morale on sports teams. Management was what I assumed impacted morale the most in Corporate America. If I saw what motivated my employees and made them happy I figured I could fix the morale.

The day before Roger returned from vacation, Todd pulled me into his office and said, "Hey man there were a few things that I forgot to tell you about. Some payment and tax information to fill out. Don't skip over the section for child support. Oh, and also your training packet." I slightly raised my voice and asked, "Child support papers?" Todd raised his hands up as if he were surrendering and said, "Whoa what's with the attitude buddy? We don't behave that way here." I don't know if I was more upset that he assumed I was on child support or that he sabotaged me from doing the work assigned to me. Todd and I split shifts. I came in at 3:00pm and he got off at 5:00pm. Todd showed me two different offices I could choose from before he left for the day. When we arrived at the first option which was directly across from the morgue I said, "Todd, I cannot be there. Please give me the other option. No matter what it is, I will take it." Todd chuckled and said, "Why not? I responded, "I had some traumatic experiences dealing with death. Under no circumstance can I stomach being across from a morgue every day." Todd put his arm around me and smiled then said, "Aw Rossy, are you scared of ghosts? I will do my best to make sure your office is not across from the big bad ghosts."

The entire commute to work the next day I wondered how I could make a great impression on Roger. On the drive to work Todd texted me, "Come straight to Roger's office when I first get in." As I approached Roger's office for the first time, my heart began to race. I heard Todd's voice in Roger's office before I could knock on the door. "How do you like the new guy?" asked a voice I never heard before. Todd responded, "I really don't know about him. He seems to have an attitude problem. I really don't know if our employees will like him." The unknown voice responded, "Interesting, has he picked out an office yet?" Todd responded, "Yes, he doesn't want to be near the cafeteria because he doesn't want to gain weight." My first impression had been made without my presence. I did not know how I could recover from a hit like that. I knocked on the office door to end their conversation and change the narrative of it. I introduced myself to the guy who had to be Roger and remained standing until he offered me a seat. "How do you like everything so far?" asked Roger. I lied and said, "It's been great. I could not ask for a better place to be. Todd has really been helping me get adjusted." Todd interjected and said, "Yes I was just telling Roger about how good I have been getting you up to speed." This muthafucka had no morals or manners. He also lacked intelligence because I was being sarcastic when I lied about how things had been going and he took it as a compliment. I don't know if lying about his treatment towards me benefited me as much as the lies he told about me benefited him.

After the meeting adjourned Roger said, "Let's go to the board meeting. I am glad you got to attend the board meetings for a few days without me being here to get an early hang of it." "What board meetings?" I asked. Roger stopped in his tracks and said, "Our daily board meeting that Todd was supposed to take you to every day since I have been gone." Todd said, "Oh yea, I couldn't find him none of those days last week when it was time to go to the meetings. He was on the other end of the hospital when it was time to go so he didn't get to go to any." Before I could even debunk Todd's lie, Roger said, "Ross I need you to be in sync with Todd when that time comes around. I can't have you missing out on board meetings because you want to chase the nurses around. When we entered the board meeting, two nurses complimented my suit. The timing couldn't be more perfect to make Roger sound as if he were right. I felt him give me a side eye when the nurses complimented me. I shouldn't have stated in the interview that I never worked around a lot of women before. My main work experience was doing construction and landscape with my dad, coaching children at sports, and selling cotton candy at New Orleans Saints and Hornets games. One of the biggest rules I had in Corporate America is to never lay where I get my pay. My ex-girlfriend made that evident to me. After the two nurses complimented my attire the whole room paid attention to my outfit. I hate attention of that nature so I humbly thanked everyone and took my seat. After the board meeting wrapped up Todd pulled me to the side and said, "I need you to tone it down. You can't be wearing clothes like that every day." My rebuttal was, "Aren't we supposed to dress professionally every day?"

Todd said, "Yes, but there is no need for you to show me and Roger up like that? You can wear a company polo, slacks, and a regular pair of loafers like me". Roger walked up and interjected, "That's a nice suit you have on? "Where did you get it from?" I answered, "Saks." Roger said, "Wow, big money." I told them I had to use the restroom so I could ease my way out of the HR unfriendly conversation.

I finally received my first paycheck after the end of my shift. The check balanced out the bullshit I had been dealt since my first day on the job. Getting handed my paycheck at the hospital was the first time I received a meaningful amount of money without having to risk my life for it. I figured this had to be the best way to get paid. This had to be what financial freedom meant. My first stop when I left work was the gas station. It took $130 worth of gas to fill the tank on my SUV. It felt weird going to the gas station and not getting a cigarillo. I could not risk failing another drug test to affect my livelihood again. I would never make the same detrimental mistake twice. I knew they could call me at any time to go urinate in a cup on the third floor. I would live a lifetime of regret if I effected my life by failing a drug test again. I had to find a new boost of happiness and coping method besides weed. As I pulled out the gas station and turned onto the nearest main street I saw my two answers. The liquor store and a buffet. I use to love going to buffets after I work out but going to a buffet after a day of work with no physical activity is a different experience for your body. I was never much of a drinker but since I didn't have weed as an option, I turned to alcohol. Over the weekend I paid off monthly bills, student loans, took care of some routine car maintenance, and purchased some groceries. I spent my entire check before it was time to go back to work on Monday.

I got a running start on the following Monday. Growing up I always saw corporate jobs as starting in the morning, so having to be at work in the afternoon was a pleasant surprise. Only thing was, I had no true plans for the morning and early afternoon. The feeling of living in a new city where you don't have any established friendships and routines is an empty one. My morning was spent working out and daydreaming about what it would be like to finally have an office. I always assumed having an office was a symbol that you had officially made it. All I could do was think about how all of the other offices looked that I had seen growing up. I always thought of offices to have a jar of candy, family pictures, and credentials to hang on the wall. All I had out of those three were a jar of candy. My credentials were in New Orleans and I didn't have any of the stereotypical family pictures.

When I arrived to work Roger met me outside of the break room to take me straight to my new office. "How was your weekend?" Roger asked as we began walking. "It was great besides spending my entire check on bills. Now I am back broke again." I responded. Roger stopped in his tracks looked at me from head to toe and said, "Broke? You don't know anything about being broke. Look at how you are dressed every day." I was befuddled Roger made that ill-advised assumption. I was even more befuddled that he passed up the office across from the cafeteria. As Roger continued to carry on about his assumption that I didn't know what being broke was I continued to keep my head on the swivel to look for where my new office would be. I zoned out and didn't hear anything Roger said, but continued to see him talk. A pause came in the conversation and Roger began to laugh hysterically. I pretended to laugh and looked at him for the next ten seconds. He then said, "You can't be an Operations Manager if you were on welfare." He then pointed at the door across from the morgue and said, "This is your new office." I covered up my displeasure from his welfare comment, but I could not cover up my displeasure after he told me my new office was across from the morgue. I looked at Roger in the eyes and said, "What do you mean this is my office? I specifically requested to not be across from the morgue." "You didn't tell me that. So I am assuming that you didn't tell Todd this either. This is your office. Deal with it. I don't care about why you don't want to be there." Roger said before he walked off. I was so pissed off. I opened up about a serious mental issue that I had with Todd and it was made a mockery of.

Todd and Roger had created hostile environments several times but I was looked at as the guilty party in their eyes. Dee, who was one of my most respected and tenured employees overheard some of my conversation with Roger. She followed me into my office as I walked in with my head down. Dee asked, "What's wrong baby?" I responded, "Todd has been messing with me and its working. Roger has been messing with me to but he is a little easier to deal with than Todd. I just had to check him though." Dee replied, "Don't be fooled by his smile. When your position opened up the last time it was between Larry and Terrance. Terrance was my boss at the last hospital I worked at before here. He left the hospital we worked at for a higher paying position with an oil and gas company. Terrance fell victim to layoffs during an Oil industry crises and couldn't get a job for over a year so he had to rely on government assistance to get by. Larry had never been a manager before and the only thing they liked about him when he was the lead housekeeper was that he told the bosses every single thing that went on with other employees. Larry had a GED and no management experience, but he still got the position over Terrance who had over a decade of management experience plus a master's degree. I overheard Roger say it would be a bad look having someone who was on government assistance working as a manager on his staff and that he didn't believe Terrance's credentials. Don't fall for their games and don't ever think there is a such thing as more evil or less evil baby. Evil is evil."

Chapter 10

Three months had gone by and I had not gained much ground financially, my health declined, and I struggled mentally. I gained fifteen pounds, developed pre-hypertension, and couldn't get stress from work out of my mind. It became harder to avoid pitfalls that I had never been taught to avoid before. Pierre was right when he said there would be no preparation for the things I would experience in Corporate America.

It was time for my first review. It felt like report card conferences in high school, but I knew the grading was subjective. On the entire commute to work I critically evaluated my performance since my first day. After evaluating the situation in its entirety, I came to the conclusion that I had done a great job, and there were no factual numbers that could prove otherwise. I had no other choice but to be confident about my first review in corporate America. I went above and beyond on every task delegated to me and my staff loved me.

When I got to my office I had a little unexpected free time because Roger was giving Todd his review first. I took the extra time to evaluate the appearance of my office and it was nothing like I had wanted it to be. It looked worse than what it was when I first got it. It looked like a storage place. There were work supplies, clothes, and items left behind by my employees spread all over. I decided to clean up and head back to my SUV to grab some things to spice up the office. As soon as I crossed the threshold of my office the hardest cries I ever heard stopped me. Out of the countless cries I ever heard, these were by far the hardest ones. I felt the cries from the opposite end of the hallway. A young woman was carrying a little black bag while being held up by a big burly man. As they walked towards my office they cried wolf tears that captured my undivided attention. The closer they got, the slower they moved. When they stopped at my office, Dee guided me the opposite way and took me around to the next hallway. When we got to the other side of the hall Dee whispered, "They just lost their newborn baby. Give them some space. Its ok, go to the gas station to catch your breath.

I will cover for you. They should have never put you by that morgue. They put every black manager across from that damn morgue and every white one by the cafeteria."

When I returned from the gas station Roger paged me on the work phone to come to his office. "Where were you?" Roger asked as soon as I walked into his office. I replied, "The gas station to grab some medicine." Roger leaned back in his chair and said, "Ok just checking. I had to make sure Dee wasn't lying to us. So how do you think your first three months went? Roger and Todd leaned forward in anticipation to hear what I had to say as if they had a surprise for me after I finished talking. I answered, "I think I did great. Our customer service feedback from patient's families was positive. The people I manage react well to me. Morale is high and I went above and beyond on every task delegated to me." Roger looked at Todd then looked at me and said, "Right, right, that is great. I agree, but I gave you a "2 out of 5" for the grade on your review. You just seem to have your head and time wrapped up into dressing to gather attention from the nurses. That was the reason you missed a week of board meetings. Also you did not take advantage of the training materials I left for you during your first week. That has been detrimental in your development. You say morale is high, but you have negatively affected the morale of the management staff with your short temper and semi-violent attitude. You have lashed out at Todd and myself on several occasions and we have those dates documented on your review. *long silence* Anything to say?" I was so shook up from seeing a mother carry her newborn child to the morgue that I was at a loss for words. I said, "Yes, thank you for the feedback. I will do everything I can to improve on what you brought to my attention. Roger responded, "Ok that was easier than we expected you to take it. Todd will give you your agenda for the rest of the shift." "You ok?" Todd asked me once we stepped outside of the office. I answered, "Yes, I'm fine. I am just sad that I let you all down." I wanted to tell him that I was sad about what I saw at the morgue, but my common sense kicked in. I kept it to myself, because he obviously didn't give a half of a fuck. Todd patted me on my shoulder and said, "Ok, great. For tonight you have to be the lead housekeeper, Maria is sick."

As much as I couldn't believe I had to watch a family carry their newborn to the morgue, I also couldn't believe I was given a 2 out of 5 on my review. Then to add insult to injury I was assigned to clean hospital beds for the rest of the night. Getting a 2 out of 5 meant I was ineligible for a raise for the next twelve months and that I could be terminated if I missed one day of work or was late two days. Maria was one of the best housekeepers on the staff. It was usually a two housekeepers to one ratio when rooms were being cleaned. Maria was the only person who wasn't assigned a partner due to how fast she worked. Todd and Roger left early that day so I had to break right into her role after the daily huddle disbursed.

Twelve jokes were made about me cleaning rooms within the first hour of filling in for Maria. It almost felt as if I were back at the oil and gas company delivering mail again. My status wasn't respected and people attempted to embarrass me because of my job duties. Two hours into my shift an influx of patients were rushed into the hospital because of an eight car wreck on the interstate nearby. It produced four fatalities and injured nine others. I called an emergency meeting with all of my staff to roll out a game plan I had constructed just in case a situation like this occurred. Planning ahead had paid off. An old man once gave me some advice of a lifetime. "Do you know what the difference is between a pilot and a passenger? Some of the passengers can figure out how to fly the plane to its destination on a perfect course with no mishaps. A pilot knows how to fly a plane through perfect conditions also. The difference is pilots know what to do if the unexpected happens and if the plane malfunctions. How often is everything perfect? Not always, right? See an experienced Pilot knows what to do in case something goes wrong. He has counters for almost everything that can happen. He is already trained for the unexpected. A passenger is not." From then on I saw myself as a pilot in every situation.

After channeling my inner Super Bowl halftime speech that I stored somewhere deep down inside of me, and rolling out a well thought out game plan I ended the meeting. Before I started back working I checked my phone because I knew I would have to put it up for the rest of the night. Todd called my cell phone twice. When I called him back he answered the phone and said, "Hey, I forgot to tell you to take the garbage out of the Nurse Practitioner's office." I said ok then let him know about everything that was going on with the influx of patients and the game plan I implemented. Todd said, "Y'all are fucked.", then quickly got off the phone.

My staff was unified for the first time. All employees were engaged with each other as we headed to execute our assignments. We all had extra tasks to do and knew we could possibly stay longer than our normal off time; however it was still all smiles. We all worked through our lunch breaks but we finished all of the rooms an hour before we were scheduled to get off. After everyone reconciled in the break room I asked them to sit right there and ran off before anyone could say a word. I came back fifteen minutes later with a hundred pieces of chicken, plenty of sides, and drinks. The rest of the night felt as if we were in the locker room celebrating after winning a championship. People who were always cutting their eyes at each other pushed all of the tables together so everyone could sit as one and enjoy the rest of the night.

When I walked through the doors the next day I felt like a coach who just won the super bowl after returning from the off season. My employees were hugging me and shaking my hand as I walked to the break room. The unity from the prior night carried on to the next day. All of the employees stood together and interacted as if they were at a family reunion. When I asked for everyone's attention the silence came about immediately. That never happened before. I felt beyond accomplished after the daily huddle was over and finally figured out what I wanted to do with my career. I wanted to work my way up through management. Not everyone has the mindset to plan for the unexpected and lead a staff as one. Those are essential abilities for a great manager. Before I started working there almost everyone hated coming to work and now everyone couldn't wait to get to work. I finally understood what it meant that people quit their manager and not their job when they leave a company.

After the huddle was over Todd told me, "Roger wants to see you in his office". As I walked in Roger's office he thumbed through some papers that were faced down on his desk. When I sat down he said, "Thank you for your efforts last night. I was called out of my sleep at 3:00am by the CEO to let me know how great of a job you did during the emergency situation." I smiled and said, "Yes I came up with a plan the day I was hired in case a similar situation occurred." It felt magnificent to finally get acknowledged for great work. Roger reached for his pen and turned the stack of papers over and said, "Great, amazing. With that being said, we have to give you your first write up because you did not take out the trash in the nurse practitioner's office that Todd asked you to before he left yesterday."

Certain pain hits you in different ways. I felt pain so many times in my life. Hurricane Katrina, seeing murders as a youth, and getting set up by my ex-girlfriend all felt different. Beauty isn't a word commonly mentioned when you think about pain. It isn't usually bought up because the hurting clouds what could be seen as beauty. The pain when you lose someone you love is inevitable, but there are things you can learn from the deceased that could be turned into beauty. You could incorporate the things that made you love them and show that love to a countless amount of people. That dead person will live on through you and others could feel from you what you felt from the person who passed on. If they died by way of tragedy it shows you how delicate our time is in life, and you could learn how to minimize your risks from falling victim to a tragic situation. If the deceased were a cause to their own demise it shows you what not to do and how you could save other lives from making the same mistakes. Pain with losing my childhood barber was very similar to me being documented one step closer to losing my job. My barber was the type of boyfriend to give a woman his undivided attention when she was and wasn't around. Bird even gave Sunny's uncle one of his kidneys to save his life. He saved her uncle's life but she helped end his. It was unthinkable that she could orchestrate his murder. I felt defeated as my barber as in the sense of what else could I do to make things work. I devised a plan that saved multiple lives months before it happened without minimal training at my job, but was still a step closer to losing my job because I did not empty a half full trash can. A great employee is hard to find in society. Most employees and applicants want the salary but don't want the grind, responsibilities, and sacrifices to be inclusive. Being that I possessed a blue collar work ethic, high level education, and uncoachable natural gifts I was led to believe I would be respected as a valuable asset by the company. Instead my entire tenure I had been stereotyped without being evaluated accordingly and continuously forced into hostile work environments. Staying after work for several hours with no overtime; working through lunch breaks; and accomplishing the unaccomplished during a life or death situation for victims were not enough for job security.

My despair was obvious over the next week. On top of being on thin ice with my job, my best friend Lamont's father passed away. Lamont's pops was my basketball trainer for over a decade. Besides the pain I felt from his death, my pain intensified that my best friend lost his father. When I didn't think the pain could get any worse it did. Lamont's dad was not an immediate blood relative so I was not able to take off for the funeral because he did not fit the requirements of bereavement leave. It's beyond me how a corporation could determine the importance of a person's funeral to an employee. I knew Lamont's dad for almost twenty years and I was not able to take one day off from work to pay my respects for his life. He was closer to me than some people who did fit the requirements for bereavement leave. I could not get that day back again in life. I never considered that I would not be able to make certain funerals depending on my relationship on paper with the deceased while I was working in Corporate America. Memories like this last way beyond when you are done working at any job. The memory is stuck with you forever and it is irrelevant to your employer. I was not sure if I wanted to deal with this restriction again in life.

Chapter 11

Several employees approached me asking about my change of mood during the week. I played it coy because I previously got burned by Todd after I opened up about something personal. Most people who asked about my mood change were being nosey and did not sincerely care. To add to the hostile environment I was working in, isolation was added to the list of things that I had to endure every day. I began missing home more than ever being that I needed to be there and I couldn't be. At the end of my shift on Thursday, I looked through my phone similar to the way when I first saw my girlfriend on social media. My cell phone had minimal recent activity. I had a plethora of unanswered text messages and social media notifications. I was hurt to see that I had missed so many texts and voicemails from Kim. As soon as I crossed the threshold of the door when I left work that Thursday night I called her.

I usually don't call anyone more than twice. If I call a second time it is to verify that my first call went through. When Kim didn't answer on the second time I called her a third time due to my shame of not being assessable for someone who I considered my best friend of the opposite sex. She finally answered on the fourth call with loud tears and cries that I felt through the phone. I instantly knew something detrimental had happened. Kim grievingly said, "My sister can't walk anymore! She can't even have children! She got the flu shot and everything went downhill. Destiny began losing feeling in her legs and is now handicapped for life. The fucked up thing is she begged our parents not to make her take it." I couldn't help but to reply with tears. When someone you love cries a new part of your body feels pain. Her sister Destiny had the body of a goddess, and now her body was crippled because of a flu shot. I sat in the car on the phone with Kim for two hours after I arrived home from the hour and fifteen minute commute. The hour and fifteen minute drive felt like three hours. After Kim vented my entire ride home, I finally revealed the pain that I had suppressed from all of the shit that I went through the past few years. Getting everything off of my chest released so much stress, but after I revealed those stories I couldn't help but think about those situations I spoke of. Did Derrick beat his charge? Is Shooter's killer still looking for me? Who else was the pastor of the mega church exploiting financially and ratting out to the crooked police? Was Jake still corrupting the city? All of these thoughts dominated my mind the entire weekend along with not being able to make my best friend's father funeral because of Corporate America.

On the following Monday eight of my employees called off. Someone was missing in each department throughout the hospital. That Monday was the emptiest I had ever seen the hospital. There had to be more patients than employees at the hospital. More people showed up last Wednesday when most of the city flooded. The break room was locked and a note was poorly taped on the door that read, "Report to the second floor."

As soon as I got to the second floor a line was wrapped all the way to the stairwell. Only one person was in line from my department, and she happened to be the last person in line. I asked her, "What's going on?" She responded, "I don't know." As we worked our way closer to the beginning of the line, I asked a guy behind me, "Do you know what we are in line for? He answered, "Yes, shots." I asked, "Tequila?" He said, "No I wish. We have to get a flu shot, and a few other ones." I laughed because I did not believe him, but when I got to the front of the line apparently he was right. Todd was sitting at a table once I got to the front of the line with papers to sign off on. I asked Todd, "What are all of these shots we have to take?" He said, "Flu, Measles, TB skin test, and another shot but I forgot the name." I responded, "Did you forget what's in all of these shots to?" He laughed and said, "I never knew." I looked at him and said, "I am not taking these shots then." He laughed and said, "Sign right here." When I rejected the pen from Todd he stood up and said, "You don't have a choice buddy." I said, "My choice has been made." Then I walked out of the room and carried on with the rest of my night. I refused to subject my body to something that has not been proven to be safe or beneficial. Kim's sister was just recently paralyzed for life from the flu shot, and plenty of employees were out sick because of it. I was already on thin ice at work and couldn't miss a day of work. Word had spread like germs that I declined the flu shot. My personal decision became public. That night a few nurses who were friends with Todd asked, "Did I think I was too good for the flu shot?" A doctor that was related by marriage to Todd approached me and said, "Wow no flu shot? Do you think you know something we all don't know?" It was ironic that almost everyone who was an ally with Todd had an unwarranted opinion about my decision to decline the shot before my shift could end. It was obvious he was running his mouth about me.

One important thing I learned from sports is that reading the rulebook is extremely important. You could win or lose the game by knowing or not knowing the rules. After Todd withheld vital training information from me I downloaded the employee handbook from the company website. On page 17 of the handbook it stated that the Flu shot (is optional) during flu season. My decision not to take the shots gave Todd motivation to lead the daily huddle at the beginning of the shift during the next day. He acted as if he had something important to say. I should have known that he only wanted to utilize this platform to be petty and to chastise me in front of my staff. He had not led a daily huddle since my first week. As he wrapped up the meeting, he said in an iniquitous manner, "I want to thank everyone who complied yesterday and got the flu shot. Now that I got that out of the way, I want to call out the one big baby who decided not to take it. He must be scared of needles or something. Ok that's it, meeting adjourned." He looked at me and smiled then walked out of the room. Every year everyone complied with the shots without question, therefore I became a rebel. All of my employees rushed to me before Todd could exit the door. Everyone talked over each other with their questions about why I declined the shot. I hate dialogues in that manner. Majority of the time when questions are asked in a reporter like manner, people hunt for headlines and make their own story. That's exactly what happened in this situation. Almost every question was, "Am I scared of needles?" Current me would have said yes because I know falsely conceding would have ended that conversation. Twenty-three year old me pridefully responded, "No, I have twelve tattoos." Suddenly the topic of conversation became my tattoos. Everyone got all bent of out shape that I was tatted because of my educational background, level of professionalism, and credentials. As if being tattoo-less would enhance my credentials. It's amazing the lengths positive people go through to cover up false negative perceptions of themselves and the lengths evil people go through to paint a false positive image to hide their dark ways.

If Roger did not want a guy who was on food stamps before working with him, I know he didn't want someone with twelve tattoos working for him. After my stance didn't budge of declining the flu shot I was delegated to wear a mask for the rest of flu season. I was prepared for my first day wearing the mask. I knew jokes were going to be coming from out of the woodworks when people saw me. My entire life I always had an arsenal of jokes that I used with no filter. If someone were brave enough to make a joke about me it would come with a disclaimer for me to chill out because they were just playing. So anytime someone saw an opportunity when they felt like they caught me slipping they would jump at the opportunity to tear me up with jokes. As soon as I walked into the break room one of my employee's Latoya asked, "Are you about to rob us with a suit and mask on boss man?" I responded, "Look like you about to rob us every day with all of that makeup you be having on." We traded jokes until it was time to start our daily huddle. After the huddle Latoya approached me and asked me to walk with her. When we got by ourselves she said, "All jokes aside, watch your back. Todd has been going around to other department heads dragging your name through the mud. He is really out to get you and he has been attempting to hit on me even though my husband works here. I have been acting friendly with him so I could get information out of him and watch his ass more closely."

When I returned back to my office, Roger was in my chair waiting for me. I asked him, "Do you need my help? He answered, "Yes, I need you to document your altercation with Latoya. We can't have her disrespecting a manager like that." I replied, "She wasn't disrespectful towards me." Roger cut me off and said, "Everybody already told me what happened, you don't have to save one of your people." It's amazing what came out of Roger's and Todd's mouth during unscripted conversations. I had to remove myself mentally from my body. I thought of something entirely different to cloud what he was saying until I heard silence. When Roger concluded his words I replied, "I am not writing her up."

Fighting to stay employed while my performance was above company standard made me forget that my birthday was coming up. My birthday is right after Christmas. I would have forgotten about my birthday if the staff did not put together a Christmas party. I was amazed that all of the employees I managed pitched in to throw a party because of how divided they were at the beginning of my tenure. A professional work environment often tends to be less mature than a typical high school environment. It was heartwarming to see that my employees graduated from putting their fingers into their colleague's food that was left unattended in the break room refrigerator to wanting to celebrate Christmas together. I had accomplished a lot at the hospital but this may have been my proudest moment. The Christmas party went better than planned. The staff invited family members, took pictures together, and created lifelong memories.

Since the day after the Christmas party was my last day working until after my birthday, my employees decided to throw me a surprise birthday party. I never had a surprise birthday party before. I was sincerely surprised that they took the effort to throw me a party. Almost the entire department attended the party. Even people not scheduled to work during the time of the party showed up. As soon as we sat down to enjoy our cake and ice cream one employee blurted out, "So boss man, how old are you by the way?" I was the last person to notice the elephant in the room because each employee's body language expressed that they had been dying to know also and they couldn't wait for me to answer the question. Several employees regurgitated the same question after I went a few seconds without responding. I said, "Y'all guess". They yelled over each other, "Thirty-five? Thirty? Forty? Thirty-One? Thirty-Two? Thirty? I was befogged by their guesses. I responded, "I am twenty-three." Their responses came in cohesion again. "No quit playing boss." You are always joking." "I know you wish you were twenty-three." "How old are you for real?" "We know you aren't in your twenties." they yelled. My distaste intensified as it became evident that they didn't believe me. "Why don't you all believe me?" I asked. "Look at you." "You have a job like this and a suit on every day." "Ain't no twenty-three year olds carry themselves like that" I think you are thirty-three." "Pull up your Facebook" they yelled a little louder. "I don't have a Facebook", I responded. Dee caught my dice. She said, "Yes you do. I tagged you in the Christmas party pictures." I pulled out my license as if I were handing it over to the police, and every one walked out of the room cursing after they read my date of birth. Party was over. "Ain't no baby fend to manage me!" "I got grandkids his age!" "Ain't no way he should have gotten this job over me!" "I'm bout to quit!" were all of the statements I heard as my employees vacated the room.

My first vacation in corporate America did not feel like an actual vacation. When you vacation from the streets, you are away from your everyday struggles. Your everyday worries such as getting arrested, and having to look over your shoulder 24/7 are not a part of your vacation. During my week long vacation all I could do was think about my everyday struggles at work. Vacation from corporate America was more stressful than taking a vacation from the streets. The word vacation no longer meant a break from every day stress. My stress hopped on the plane with my luggage and traveled with me back to New Orleans.

There were no major adjustments that I could think of to make, and I had given it my all. Not being able to self-medicate due to company policy only made my stress levels skyrocket. Having traces of THC in your system had no correlation to job performance however your employment would be terminated if it were present in your system. If anything employees would perform better if they were able to smoke leisurely while they were away from work. One may be quick to say someone shouldn't come to work high on weed, but that is not what I said. An employee being able to enjoy alcohol and not weed during their off time is illogical. Before working at the hospital I didn't even drink enough to be considered a social drinker. In college I went over two years without drinking which is equivalent to ten years in real life.

101

Drinking alcohol on a weekly basis became an escape after days of work to cope with the stress. My health had also deteriorated. For the first time in life I was no longer completely healthy. My coping methods for stress raised my blood pressure to hypertension level at the age of twenty-three.

The only thing I had going for me at work was my relationships with the people I managed and I was unsure if my relationships with them would ever be the same after they found out my age. It is mental betrayal when someone who should be happy for you isn't. It was incomprehensible how quick they flipped on me. After two weeks of buying lunches and ego stroking most of my employees were back on my side. The two most tenured employees were the only holdovers who still showed spite towards me. I had to pretend like I understood their pain. The absence of Dee's support hurt the most. She was one person who I thought I could be cool with outside of work. After the daily huddle Dee pulled me aside and said, "I'm sorry. I have been stressed out with other things outside of work lately. Then after I found out your age it made me reflect on my journey. I got sad about the things I didn't accomplish in my past that I should have. I can't do nothing but be proud and happy for you young man. You have a bright future and I will do whatever I can to help you get there." The thing about relationships is that ones which are willing to work through problems are to be deemed as valuable. A relationships true value will be assessed accurately when a disagreement, miscommunication, or conflict comes about. This situation made me and Dee closer than before. Maria was the last employee who was still being standoffish with me, so I decided to approach her after my conversation with Dee concluded. When I approached Maria with an apology which was not even well warranted, she pretended as if she did not know English too well. Maria had done an excellent job of pretending not to know English when she did not feel like talking. Only thing is, no one can act every day for thirty years. The truth will seep out. Her game was well known and she still continued to run it effectively. After five minutes of getting nowhere close to a common ground with Maria I decided to continue on with my shift.

Every time I had a vacation break from school I came back refreshed and ready to go back to work. I had a fake excitement to be back at work. After the conversation with Maria I could not even fool myself that I was happy to be back. That day each hour until lunch felt like a day. My hour lunch only felt like a few minutes. Things began to loosen up for me once I realized I was off in a few hours. As I tried to convince myself that the rest of my shift would go great my work phone rang. It was the charge nurse from the ICU. If I received a call from a charge nurse it was usually due to a housekeeper not executing their job correctly. I rarely got a call from the ICU nurses because Maria usually handled her business correctly every night. The charge nurse said, "Hey we need help up here immediately. Maria is nowhere to be found and we need ICU rooms cleaned ASAP for patients being transported from the ER." I called Maria several times but she did not respond so I decided to sneak up on her. Maria gave off a strong scent that reeked of cigarettes and body oils that smelled like she got them from a barbershop. I was able to sniff her out on the ICU floor. She was hiding in the bathroom of a hospital room that was used for storage. Game was on as soon as I approached. She began to mumble curses at me in Spanish but little did she know I was one year removed from 500 level Spanish classes at a top university. I played her game and began to speak to her in English. Her first three profanity laced rebuttals were in Spanish refusing to go back to work. So I decided to ask my fourth and fifth questions in Spanish. She became silent after I defeated her at her poorly played game. I went back to my office to begin typing up a write up for her. I called Roger to ask him a general question about the documentation process because it was my first time administering one. It was obvious he was proud of me for finally writing a person up. After he walked me through the process on how to write someone up he asked, "Who are you writing up?" When I told him Maria the direction of his narrative changed. "Shred that document. You know how Maria is. She is our best worker. Let that go." Roger said. "Insubordinate and disrespectful, yes I know how she is. She also cursed at me in Spanish several times." I responded. "You don't understand Spanish. Shred the document now and get back to work." Roger said then hung up the phone.

I was back living in a state of paranoia. I didn't know how I could get through the next few years at this job. During my dark days at the oil and gas company I regretted accepting that position, and going to college. After being away from college I realized the most important things I learned from college were the importance of relationships, work ethic, and time management. I had a better view on college after I was removed from it. I also did not notice what I learned about my previous position until I was removed from the situation. The oil and gas job showed me the importance of perseverance and professionalism. My entire college career I thought I was guaranteed a high paying job if I graduated. Working for $9 an hour after I received my college degree humbled me permanently. I felt the oil and gas position was an end all be all because I did not have a plan to make it out of the situation. I still respected the job enough to show up every day on time and executed my job duties which I was extremely overqualified for. Because of my perseverance to find another opportunity I found my career. My professionalism earned me a solid reference from the oil and gas company that helped me get the position at the hospital. During my tenure at the hospital I was blinded of what my takeaways would be and what I would appreciate about that journey.

For the next few months I felt as if I were dodging raindrops at the hospital. Todd and Roger attempted to put me into several situations that could potentially result in another write up. After being burned out from dodging raindrops my only option was to involve Human Resources. I always looked at going to HR the same way the streets look at snitching. A snitch was something I had the least respect for, and so did everyone on the streets in my era. Any man who would tell on another man who took the same risk as him is void of any integrity and loyalty. I never thought Roger would fire me but I just wanted the negative documentation rescinded. Corporate America forced me to go against my life principals and morals. As I sat in the office with the Human Resources manager, Todd, and Roger, I began to feel uncomfortable in my own skin. I could not recognize myself as I began to voice my displeasure of how I was treated by Roger and Todd. After my first two sentences the Human Resources manager began to cut me off every other sentence. This avocado seed head woman was listening to respond instead of to comprehend. I was never allowed to fully explain anything for the first five minutes so I decided not to let this gathering make it to its sixth minute. Justice was not served by the person who was hired to serve it. Even if I reached out to go over their head, the unwritten code of retaliation would be in full effect. Once word got out that I went to HR I knew I would become that guy who none of my colleagues or higher-ups wanted to work with, and people would side with the wrong doers instead of me.

When I woke up the next morning I felt extremely sick. For some reason I still toughed it out and went to work. I could not breathe out my nose for anything so I decided not to wear my mask. After I sat down in the break room almost everyone approached me with get well soon gestures because I was obviously sick. "Put that mask back on buddy. I don't care if you can't breathe. It's company policy," Todd said. "Ok well I'm headed back home," I responded. "If you do I will count that as an unexcused absence", Todd said. I got up and started with the daily huddle. Todd called to see if Roger was in his office while I was leading the meeting then left out and didn't come back in. Todd and Roger leaving early was a significant relief. I was looking forward to the rest of the night. The rest of the night went by smoothly until two hours before the end of the shift.

ICU was calling again. Maria was nowhere to be found for the past two hours and ICU had a rush of patients from the ER. I stuck my nose in the air and sniffed for the scent of cheap perfume for about fifteen minutes but to no avail. The ICU charge nurse began to blow my phone up again. When I answered an infuriated voice came across the phone, "We need these rooms cleaned immediately!" It was impossible for me to clean these rooms by myself within the amount of time they wanted them cleaned by. I grabbed Dee to help me with the rooms and an extra nurse decided to pitch in and help us. One impossible situation is doable, but two is a different story. I knew we could clean the rooms in a timely manner but I knew it was impossible to make it back to the break room for the transition of the second and third shift. It was essential that I was there in the break room for the end of the second shift and the beginning of the third shift. During transition time I was responsible for making sure the second shift employees returned all of their equipment. I was also responsible for briefing the third shift on their job responsibilities. While the second shift may seem like the most urgent priority out of the two, the third shift was by far more urgent. My second shift employees were placed on that shift selectively due to their tenure and performance. The third shift was quite the opposite. The turnover rate was worse than a temp service. A new person quit almost every week and it took more than a month to find a new person to hire. There were mainly three types of problems on the overnight shift. Accountability, because no one was there to watch them besides the first hour of their shift so people would get caught on camera sleeping, or sneaking out of work almost every week. The quality of candidates was the second problem. Most of the applicants applied because they couldn't find a job anywhere else during the day due to their record or lack of credentials. Three was the overnight employees felt like outlaws because they missed everything company related and barely had any communication with their first and second shift colleagues.

I received over fifteen calls from my employees once it was

five minutes until transition time because I was not in the break room for something I was always there for and took so serious. Since only one room was left undone I decided to run downstairs to the break room to handle the transition. Before I got back to the break room I sent one employee on the third shift directly upstairs to clean the one remaining room. When I made it to the break room almost everyone was mad at me and Maria was still nowhere to be found. "Where is Maria?" I asked the room. She put her cart up and left about thirty minutes ago several people responded. The ICU charge nurse continuously rang my phone while I was handling the transition. My employee from the third shift that cleaned the room in the ICU had made it back downstairs after the transition was over and told me, "They are fuming. You might not want to go up there." She was right. I had already apologized and did everything I could do to get the job done. There was nothing else I could do.

When I arrived to work the next day there were police and security guards at every door of the hospital near the break room. I was nervous because it seemed like a tragic event might have occurred. After I made it to the door where I usually entered the hospital I asked the security guard, "What happened?" He responded "Nothing, just part of a procedure". Cool, I was relieved. Todd was waiting for me outside of the break room. "This way sir", he instructed me. "You don't want me to start the huddle?" I replied. "No need to. Walk with me to Roger's office," Todd said. Roger was laid back in his chair while he thumbed through a stack of papers turned down on his desk. I sat down without saying anything. Roger cracked the few seconds of silence, "So, what happened last night?" I responded, "We had an emergency situation in the ICU. Maria was insubordinate again and went missing, so we had to complete her rooms during the emergency. I actually cleaned her assigned rooms along with Dee and another nurse." Roger squinted his eyes then asked, "Are you leaving out anything?" I didn't know what else I could have left out but I reached, and said "Yes I was extremely sick but I still made it through." Roger took a deep breath then said, "Ok, well I hate that it has to be like this, but we have to part ways. You have been quite combative with me and Todd since you began here. You started off on a bad note by not using the training materials I left for you on your first week. Your employees do not respect you. That's why Maria won't listen to you. Also you were selfish when you decided to go against the grain and decline the shots. That is a stain on our department. The final straw was last night when I got a call from the ICU charge nurse saying that you did not get the rooms cleaned in a timely manner." From day one fundamental information about my job was hidden from me. Throughout my tenure I still over performed without proper tutelage from my managers. My managers continually racially stereotyped me and tried to correlate that with my performance. I was also not allowed to do my managerial duties. I had to pick and choose who I could write up depending on their ethnicity. Consequently there were no repercussions for employees being insubordinate. If someone is not punished for their actions it is deemed as acceptable. You are the reason why it was acceptable for Maria to be insubordinate with me. I had all of this prepared for a rebuttal in my head, but I decided to leave it in my head and didn't say anything in return. The verdict had been made, it was their words verses mines. Here was a place that wasn't worth fighting for. After Roger said his last word, Todd and him acted as if they were scared of my reaction. Their body language assumed that they expected I would attack them verbally, and physically. "Thank you for the opportunity and God bless", I told them as I rose out of my chair that I pushed back under the table. I looked at each one of them dead in their eyes so I could see through there soul. My eyes were mirrors that gave them a self-reflection to see how phony they were when they looked in my eyes. They won the battle but lost the war. Having to win by playing dirty is not a true victory. The mental conscious will not free itself enough to cherish the joy of victory. One who gave it their all will still win in defeat because they know they did everything in their power to win. Their mind will be eased by concluding that they did everything within their capabilities to win. That original battle may not be the ultimate victory. The next battle after defeat will be the true championship game. That victory will be sweeter than the one initially planned.

Chapter 12

God did not close one door without opening up several more. I had a new found energy and confidence after my tenure at the hospital. I was disappointed about not progressing financially from my previous position but I was elated that it solidified my résumé. I knew money would be on the way soon. Getting fired did something to my soul. Taking a break from working wasn't an option because I had such a fire in me to show Roger and Todd that they missed out on a great thing. I got fired on a Monday evening and was up Tuesday morning at 6:00am looking for jobs. My sense of urgency was thirty times higher than it was when I was looking for jobs at the oil and gas company. Previously I felt it was impossible to match that determination, better yet out do it. My approach looking for jobs was great during that time, but I decided to step it up even harder on this go around. A face to face interaction is a million times better than applying online and waiting for a call. There was a job fair later that day and I was not going to miss it even if I found out about it last minute.

Almost every company there was a Fortune 500 company. When I got to the job fair I decided to get straight to the point. Oil and gas companies were to the left of the room. The financial companies were to the back left. The cell phone companies were straight back. The healthcare companies were back right, and automotive companies were to the right. I initially moved to Houston to get in the oil and gas industry, but I wound up getting the worse job the oil and gas industry had to offer. I felt I was more than worthy for a good entry level position now. I made my way to the oil and gas section and I was not warmly welcomed. Almost each company asked would it be a problem cutting my beard, and were not focused on asking what I could provide as an employee for their company. It felt as if I were dealing with a bunch of Todd and Rogers all over again. They were more concerned with my appearance than my experience. I did not stay at the oil and gas section long. My first semester in college cancelled my finance dreams. I squeaked out of finance 101 my freshman year with a D minus. The teacher only passed me because I showed up to every class and she thought I was funny. Needless to say my finance journey ended there and I passed that section up. I never wanted to work with electronics and cell phones because I felt I didn't have enough control over the devices. Conversations were short lived at that section. My surety of leaving with a job or a job interview had plummeted. Needless to say I skipped the healthcare table also. Seeing the healthcare section made me zone out and head to the exit.

A middle aged woman, who appeared to be the aunt in the family that everyone loved left her table and stood in my way to stop me from passing her booth up. When I looked up after she stopped me in my footsteps she asked, "How are you doing? It looks like you have a lot on your mind?" Usually when people ask "How are you doing?" it is the same as saying hello. Almost everyone responds good even when things are going terrible. I felt the sincerity when she asked me that question. "I am not doing so well", I responded. She immediately replied, "I don't know what has you feeling down but hopefully knowing that I think you would be a great candidate for an open position with our company will make you feel better." I didn't even notice the name of the company she represented but she put a smile on my face. Her greeting had me so caught off guard that I did not notice I didn't respond until she said, "It's a great opportunity that could teach you how to run a business and also your performance will control your upward mobility with the company." After I missed my best friend's father funeral was the first time I thought about owning my own business. I figured that might be the perfect opportunity where my performance wasn't subjective and to learn how to run a business in case the next corporate opportunity didn't work out. "What is the next step?" I asked the recruiter. "It's three rounds of interviews. Your first interview is with me. I will call you this evening to set up an interview for tomorrow. I am looking forward to talking to you later." she responded. I shook her hand and thanked her then walked off. She was one of the few friendly people that I met in corporate America. She could have been offering me one of the worst jobs in the world, but her sincerity which was something no one had showed me so far in the work world made me want to work wherever she was at. When I got to my car, and finally looked at her card my mood was killed because the opportunity was at a rental car company.

A rental car company very well may have been the last place I ever thought I would work. The oil and gas opportunity was less farfetched than a rental car company. However the vibe I got from their recruiter and the chance to learn how to run a business left me intrigued. My entire life before I met Uriah I was late for almost everything no matter the importance. Ever since being an understudy of his I learned to put an extra level of respect on other people's time and showed up significantly early when I was meeting with someone else. I arrived to the interview twenty minutes early and took a seat in the lobby. This interview was much different from when I was at the hospital. I was meeting at a true corporate office and no one was anticipating my arrival besides the person I was meeting with. There was barely anyone in the lobby while I waited and the people that walked by were very brief if they said anything at all. It gave me an extra sense of motivation because I was barely acknowledged as I waited. The recruiter greeted me with the same warm smile she gave me at the job fair and led me to her office. During the interview she asked me more

111

questions about my personal life and then went on to ask me about my work experience. Once she felt me out as a person I think her decision was made. She concluded the interview by saying, "I am not supposed to be telling you this yet, but I will schedule an interview with the area manager closest to the address on your application tomorrow. Be ready, and good luck. That night I over prepared for my interview with the area manager. During the interview the recruiter sold me on something else that intrigued me. The managers with the company are more inclined to develop their employees because the people they manage performance greatly affects their paychecks. Todd and Roger had no inclination to help me.

The commute to my second interview was significantly shorter than my commute to the hospital. The drive was only eight minutes away from my house. Those long drives to my previous job gave me extra time to prepare when I left the house but the ride to the interview went by so fast that I felt a tad bit rushed when I arrived to my destination. When I got to the branch it was a packed house and the area manager I would be interviewing with was not there yet. Getting there early gave me some time to relax and observe the new environment. The flow of business at the branch was something I was never exposed to. Going from sitting behind a desk delegating to a fast paced sales environment was a transition that made me edgy. My plans for this job was not long term so my nerves were settled quickly when I reminded myself of that. A short guy who looked extremely young to be an area manager approached me and said "Welcome. Come into the office. My name is Shane. I am the area manager that will be conducting your second round interview. You played college basketball right?" "Yes sir I played for a few years." I responded as I took a seat in his office. Shane said, "Wow I'm amazed that you were on a college basketball team and you aren't even six feet tall. That says a lot about your heart and personality." The rest of the conversation was mainly about sports. I was impressed how he correlated sports to work environments. Most of his questions were asking how I could apply what I learned from sports to work. Shane and the recruiter had learned more about me in one conversation than what Roger and Todd learned about me in almost one year. When the area manager offered to walk me to my car I was sure that I was successful in this round of interviews also. Before we parted ways he smiled and said, "Be ready for the championship, Friday. You meet with the regional vice president. He is going to grill you a little but that is more of the confirmation interview. He just wants to meet who we are bringing on." I thanked him then pulled off. I wanted to celebrate but I knew it was not the appropriate time yet. I was nervous every hour leading up to the third round interview. I had performed well in every step of the interview process and I did not want to mess it up on my final round.

On my second visit to the corporate office things changed from the first time I waited in the lobby. While I waited for my third interview more people acknowledged me. A woman who introduced herself as the secretary for the Regional Vice President asked me to follow her to his office. The Regional Vice President came off as the stereotypical CEO. He was sitting with his back turned to the door and spun his chair around when I entered his office. He then stood up and introduced himself and asked me to have a seat. I was in awe because of his polish and demeanor. He happened to be from New Orleans also so that loosened up my initial uptight vibe. After about ten or fifteen minutes of leisurely based conversations, he hit me with questions that caught me off guard. They caught me so far off guard that I wasn't even sure if I still came off as deserving of the job. Immediately after I gave my answer to his final question he sharply said, "The interview is over.", then walked me to the door before I could respond. As I crossed the threshold of his office he said, "If we go in your direction or another we will call you to let you know what we decide."

I initially had plans to go out that weekend but canceled them because I was not in the mood to party anymore. I felt I might have blown my opportunity to get hired. The three day weekend felt like three weeks. That following Monday I received three job offers from other companies, but still didn't hear back from the rental car company. It felt like every girl wanted me besides the one I really wanted. On Tuesday I refreshed my emails every five minutes and checked my phone every thirty seconds for them to follow up with me. After I did not hear from them by 1:00pm on Tuesday I decided to head to the gym to ease my mind. As soon as I veered onto the interstate my phone rang. I knew it was the rental car company before I even looked at my phone. I pulled to the shoulder when I saw it was them on the caller ID. I was so anxious that I almost let the incoming call turn into a missed call. When I answered the phone the Regional Vice President asked, "How do you think you did on the final interview?" I replied, "I think I did well besides the few questions I stumbled on." He responded, "I think you struggled the entire interview. *brief silence* I am joking man sorry for pulling your leg. You did an amazing job. I always do that to the candidates I really like. Plus you are from my hometown. Welcome to the company." I thanked him about four times then hung up and merged back onto the interstate. I had to self-check myself after we got off the phone, because initially this was a position that I did not want, but now it was a journey that I was looking forward to.

Chapter 13

My excitement of landing the position at the rental car company did not make me forget that this was only a temporary job until I found something more prestigious. My first week at the job reminded me of why I saw this as a temporary stop in my journey. The first week my responsibilities were to clean vehicles and to give customers rides to and from the branch. Each car ride was a knock on my pride. Customers asked me such questions as, "Why did you go to college if you are giving rides for a living? What do you want to be when you grow up?", and offered me tips out of sympathy. My high wore down from being excited about the new journey before the end of my first week on the job. The second week introduced me to the culture of sales. A sales environment reminded me of sports. May the best players win. I attended a week long training in a classroom setting with fifteen other employees. A hierarchy was quickly put into place. There were five people in my class who seemed remedial and that they wouldn't make it to the end of their first month. Four other people stood out besides myself, and the rest were mediocre. Being looked at as one of the best new hires in my training class ignited my competitive spirit. Four other new hires and I placed a bet that whoever got promoted first would win $500. Each of us had to put up $100. I knew I could not earn the fastest promotion by washing cars and giving rides so, some things had to change when I got back to the branch after training.

On my first day back from training everyone else in my branch was working as if they placed a bet also. Colleagues were doing anything to get sales, even if it meant stepping on another employee's toes. This team environment was really every man for himself in a free for all. I did not get my first opportunity to work with a customer until my second day back.

Caroline was assigned to train me until I got the hang of everything. Instead of training me she only focused on getting her sales. A woman of licorice skin tone that had on poorly cleaned clothing entered the store and asked for Caroline. When Caroline asked, how she could help her, the customer responded that she just wanted the cheapest deal. Caroline then pointed at me and said, "Ok he will help you." I almost threw up when Caroline passed the customer onto me as if the customer had no value. It was very reminiscent of how I was treated when I asked to be helped at retail stores when employees didn't believe I could afford what they were selling. This was the first time I was on the other end of the spectrum so I was extremely motivated to service the customer as best as possible. The customer's anger went away when I replaced Caroline in the cycle of service and took over the transaction.

I greeted the customer as if I were serving her food at a family reunion. After she reiterated that she wanted the cheapest deal I guided her outside to the lot of cars in the front of the store. We carried on a personable conversation as we walked the lot of cars. After five minutes of building rapport with her I said, "All of the vehicles in the front lot are reserved. The available vehicles are in the back lot. Let me pull around the vehicle that fits what you asked for." I went to the back lot and pulled around a hatchback car with four seats and three door handles which was our cheapest car. I did not know what her purpose for renting was but it felt similar to when I put Caron on. He wanted the cheapest thing but the cheapest thing wasn't the most beneficial thing for him. As I turned into the front lot I saw her smile turn upside down and she was visibly frustrated. Once I saw her disappointment, I knew I had a sale on my hands.

"Rule 1" Of sales is to agree with the customer before you rebuttal with something to convince them against what they came for. Before my left foot hit the ground she raised her voice and said, "Hell no baby. I am not riding my three kids and husband to my class reunion in this little bitty piece of shit. "Rule 2" Leave a few seconds of silence after you think a customer may be done speaking. The last thing you want to do is cut them off when they may be talking themselves into a sale. The brief silence also gives them time to reflect on what they just said, and gives you time to prepare the most efficient rebuttal. After a few seconds I broke the silence and asked her, "Does your high school do two year class reunions?" "Rule 3" In sales is always look for an opportunity to make them laugh and compliment them without forcing it. Forcing a joke will give off the vibe of a cheesy car salesman and insincerity. She responded, "You are sweet baby, but this is my twenty year class reunion." "Rule 4" Is to fact find. How are you going to sell someone on something if you don't know the details of the customer's needs and wants? "Which city is the reunion in?" I asked. After she replied, "Jackson, Mississippi" I did the math of the commute from Houston, Texas to Jackson, Mississippi. There was no way this lady who was built like a jar of honey was going to ride in a hatchback car for eight hours. "Rule 5" Is to paraphrase. Her needs made it evident that she had not thought her initial plan all the way through. In a rhetorical manner I asked her, "So you want to ride eight hours with four other people and pull up at your class reunion in this car?" She shook her head no and I said, "Let me get you something that will be perfect for you." I went to the back lot and pulled around a brand new Sports Utility Vehicle. Her face and body language was the opposite of when I pulled around the hatchback car. While I pulled around the SUV the customer cheered as if she were a cheerleader and I was a running back nearing the end zone. "Rule 6" Create a sense of urgency. Anytime someone is shopping and sees that supplies are limited a customer is more inclined to buy. Creating a sense of urgency is one of the most effective marketing schemes. In most cases when a company says supplies are limited they are well stocked on the product. I created the same sense of urgency. When I got out of the SUV I told the customer, "This is the last SUV left. I am surprised this vehicle is still available on a day like this." Not only did I sell her on spending additional money on an upgraded vehicle. I also sold her on buying additional protection to avoid liability for damages to the vehicle, and two other additional ancillary items. Caroline had been the top seller in the region for four months running. I thought little of her abilities after she walked away from a sale like that. Her stereotypical and ignorant mindset cost her a great sale. My drive to outshine her was more desirable than winning the $500 from the bet. I hated every employee like her growing up and would damned if I let someone like that outperform me.

I blazed through the next three months with that same passion and placed top five out of hundreds of employees in the region. The competitive professional environment was the feeling I looked for during my internship at the courthouse. Being in a sales environment gave me the opportunity to compete again, which was something that I drastically missed. Several higher paying oil and gas opportunities were presented to me in that timeframe but they did not garner my interest. If you are the best at anything in life it will prove to be lucrative. Having immaculate success so early in my tenure with no previous experience made me feel that the sky was the limit with the rental car company. I saw myself there for decades to come.

My initial goal of winning the $500 was small change compared to what I worked myself into. The next promotion was $15,000 more than my current salary. My branch manager was up for a promotion also. His increase would be an extra $30,000. Not only was his promotion worth twice as much as mines. He was twice more focused on getting himself promoted than training me. The revenue I generated helped put him in the position to get promoted so all he wanted me to do was focus on driving sales. Anytime I asked him for knowledge on marketing, analytics, or customer service he told me to only focus on sales. If I remained only focused on sales then I would fail at the next level, assistant manager. If I failed as an assistant manager that would be on me, not him. Halfway through my third month my area manager had a mental telepathy. He decided to transfer me to a different store in his area. I was skeptical at first because people told me my sales would suffer because my new branch was inside of a car dealership. Truth is about sales, if you are a great salesperson you can sell anywhere. Shane explained that to me and ensured that the next part of his plan was for me to learn how to run a business.

Gerald, my new branch manager taught me more in four days than I learned the previous four months. The first month we worked together both of us finished the month ranked in the top three for our respective positions. At the end of each month the top performers in the region are taken to an event called, heavy hitters. Heavy hitters was an award ceremony with a field trip type atmosphere. I figured anyone who consistently won awards would capitalize on the upward mobility the company had to offer. That did not correlate with my branch manager's reality. I rode with Gerald to the heavy hitters event. During the ride he told me that he finished #1 several times every year, and had been in the same position for eight years. My previous branch manager had just got promoted to area manager and had only been in his position for two years. Also my previous branch manager only finished #1 twice. Asking a person why they haven't accomplished something isn't a question you want to ask shortly after meeting them. That didn't stop me from trying to figure out why he hadn't got promoted to a higher position in eight years when he was more than deserving.

When we got to the event all of the higher ups bragged about him to me and my other colleagues. Paul was the only other area manager I knew besides Shane. After my second time at heavy hitters Paul began recruiting me to his area. I saw Paul as my best option to find out why Gerald hadn't been moved up yet. Paul treated me to a drink at every company wide event that we were both in attendance. When we sat down to drink I asked, "Why hasn't my branch manager been promoted if he has been a top performer for so many years?" Paul replied, "It's not about what you do. It's about who you know, and who you have relationships with. You can be a top performer but if you aren't in the right person's ear then someone who is in the right person's ear will get promoted before the top performer." It made zero sense to me. I tried my best not to envision that happening to me so I changed the subject. My area manager walked up as soon as he spotted me and Paul drinking. He joined our conversations every time he saw us together. Shane pulled me away as if he had something urgent to tell me and said, "You might want to limit your time around him". When I asked "Why is that?" His response was very vague and did not tell me exactly why. Maybe he sensed that Paul was recruiting me to his area. He was right. Paul had sold me on a position that would be opening up in his area soon and told me I would be a shoe in when it opened up. For the remainder of my time with Gerald I decided to watch him day by day to see why he wasn't getting promoted. After working with him for over a month, I watched higher ups shower him with compliments, observed his sky high integrity, and his great management skills. His excellent tutelage helped me earn a promotion to assistant manager in record time. Maybe it was his skin color that held him back.

Shane attempted to persuade me to stay in his area and turn down the promotion but it would have taken more than the vague reasons he offered for me to turn down a $15,000 annual raise. During the interview with Paul he spent an uncomfortable amount of time stroking my ego. He let me know I had the position before the interview was over. The fact that I was going to the lowest performing store in the region did not scare me away from accepting the position. The branch had a negative operating profit, and was last in customer service scores. Almost everyone in the company thought I made a bad decision to accept the position because it seemed impossible to turn the store around. I saw turning the store around as an opportunity to impress my higher ups and earn respect amongst my colleagues.

Chapter 14

My first day was everything as advertised plus more. My manager would go against company policy for boxes of chicken. All of the employees hated coming to work, and customers did not respect the operation. As much as I wanted to take over the business immediately, that was not the best strategy. I sat back and took note of what was wrong with the operation and devised a plan to fix it. There were two bright sides to this situation. My branch manager told me on her first day that she would be quitting soon, and my manager trainee was by far the hardest working person I ever managed. I decided to take him under my wing. This was the first time I had an opportunity to display my developmental skills at the company. My first order of action was to study him and see what his strengths and areas of improvements were. My previous area manager warned me that my new branch manager might be the worst manager in the region and advised me to learn what not to do from her. I wondered why he specifically warned me about her and not Paul. He acted as if it were a secret.

Shane was correct about my new manager. Her sales process and professionalism was the worst I had ever seen in my life. She would greet the customer in an unwelcoming manner and then complete most of the transaction. Next she would call one of the employees to take the customer outside which was the final part of the transaction. The salesperson had no chance to fact find and build solid rapport which are arguably the two most important steps of the sales cycle. Somehow Josh was still able to close a respectable amount of his deals. The mindset I had towards managing Josh was to develop him to be better than me. Every manager I had in my career besides Gerald were intimidated by my potential and did nothing to foster my growth as an employee. After I watched Josh execute several things I taught him, it became evident to me that helping someone else succeed was one of the most rewarding feelings of my job.

Two months under Gloria's management had been detrimental in Josh's success. She did not let me implement any changes I wanted to make. I could not let another day go by with him in that rinky dink system. I pulled my manager aside and asked could I treat her to lunch and sent her to go pick it up. A dark three piece with a side of fries got her to leave the office. After she left I asked Josh to shadow me on a customer for the entire sales process. Luckily the customer's situation was similar to my first one with the company and I was able to execute the sales process perfectly. My sales culture was now implemented in the branch.

Josh pushed his way from being ranked #47 in sales to being ranked #4 at the end of my third month managing him. Sales are only a portion of what makes you promotable from the manager trainee position. Five factors go into the overall rankings. Three are based on individual performance and two are based on the store's performance. You have to finish in the top 33% overall in your position for 3 out of 6 months to be promotable. Josh had not been close to qualifying in previous months because of the store's poor performance and Gloria's horrible sales process. I helped Josh improve his individual numbers, but unfortunately I had minimal impact on the store's overall numbers.

The individual sales numbers were finalized the last day of each month. The overall rankings weren't finalized until a week later. Being that Josh placed fourth in sales out of over a hundred employees we felt he definitely would finish in the top 33% for the first time. The day before the final rankings came out Josh and I decided to go celebrate after we got off. We decided to hit up the local wing shop around the corner, and had about five drinks each. Bonding with Josh bought me to the realization that I had only made one friend in Corporate America. Most people in Corporate America were too unhappy with their jobs and insecure about their job security to befriend anyone. I went into that dinner with the mindset of keeping it work related, but we opened up beyond that and it was a relieving feeling. Work had been mental isolation for me and now I had someone I could relate to. Isolation is one of the worst experiences of all time. My mind was a mental prison. Being in solitary confinement in prison is known to be ten times worse than being in general population. Jail may be the worst place on earth. That just speaks volumes of how tragic being in isolation can be.

I arrived to work early the next morning in anticipation to break the great news to Josh about him finishing in the top 33%. After I saw the final rankings I no longer anticipated telling Josh where he finished overall. He finished two spots below the top third. I wanted to leave work after I read the final rankings. Only problem was, Josh and I were the only people at work that morning. I had to sit there for thirty minutes by myself trying to figure out how I was going to break the news to him. When he walked in I didn't have to say a word for him to know. I could not hide the look on my face and he asked, "I didn't make it?" I replied, "No my brother, but…" He slammed my office door before I could finish my optimistic viewpoint. Josh yelled, "Fuck this man! I then wasted several months in this bitch. I spent a few months learning nothing, then I get properly trained and still fail because of some shit I didn't have control over. I don't give a fuck bro. I'm out." Josh peeled off in his car and left me at work alone. I had to work by myself until 3pm when Tiffany got out of school. I didn't blow his phone up when he left. He deserved some time to himself. It hurt me that he went so hard every day and had nothing to show for it. I decided to put that energy and motivation into my work to show him that we could succeed in this company. I made the company a record amount of money in sales that morning because of my pain for Josh. Before I knew it Tiffany walked through the door and I could finally take my first break of the day. Josh's situation made me disregard my individual ranking that morning. I fell victim to the store's performance also. My personal numbers were high, but I did not finish in the top 33% because of some numbers I had no control of.

Josh did not call that Thursday night so I was worried about him not showing up to work the next day which was the busiest day of the week. That Friday I got to work at 6:15am to start washing cars to get ahead for the day. When I arrived at the branch, lights were on in the back of the building. I crept around the side closest to the wash bay and saw that Josh was already into a full sweat washing cars. He already cleaned four cars before the sun came up. Capturing that moment made me realize how important it was to have the right people on your team. Josh's will to fight through adversity set the tone that we would fight through anything to accomplish our goals. That resilient mindset rubbed off throughout the entire branch. Tiffany who was on the verge of putting in her two weeks before my first day was now fully vested in the branch. She previously stepped down from being a manager trainee to a part-time employee to further her education. Gloria's resignation couldn't have come at a better time. She was the only one with a negative vibe in the branch.

Having three different managers in five months was a new experience for me. Consistency and a constant voice of direction are important parts of any relationship, both personal and business. Keep having to start over can be mentally draining. Now it was on to my fourth manager in four months. After a week of anticipating who my next manager would be I received some unexpected news. No one applied for the position. The store's poor performance over the past few years, and the neighborhood the branch was in scared everyone away from applying for a 10% raise on their annual salary. Paul spent off my informal promotion as if it wasn't a fallback plan. It was a worst case scenario decision, but I never mix my feelings with business so I felt no type of way about that besides motivated.

I had only been with the company for eight months but now I was responsible for managing several employees, a 200 car fleet, and an operation that generates over one million dollars monthly. If it wasn't for Gerald's tutelage I would not have been ready for this opportunity. I had a basic knowledge of the business but an advanced motivation to turn my branch around. Paul added some fire to my fuel and told me that, "If Josh and I could turn the store around then I would get promoted to branch manager at the store and Josh would take my spot as assistant manager.

Each day Josh and I worked as if we had a $15,000 promotion on the line because we did. For three months straight we continued to show up to work early, leave late, and improve every day. Paul told us to keep our extra efforts between me, himself, and Josh. Only a few other people knew how hard we worked and they called us insane. Anytime you are in pursuit of excellence or a goal that others haven't achieved you will deal with heavy scrutiny.

Our workload increased to working every weekend, and seventy hours a week. The extra work Josh and myself put in delivered the branch to prominence. We both finished top three overall and Paul finished as the top area manager. He hadn't finished first in two years. Our performance was instrumental in helping him finish first. All of us were invited to the Heavy Hitters event for that month. This was the first time I saw Gerald since we worked together at the same branch. We spent the entire awards ceremony catching up. This was the third time he finished #1 in the previous five months but was still passed on for a promotion two times during that time span. Conversation picked up when they called my area manager up to receive his award. "How did y'all turn the store around?" Gerald asked as Paul headed towards the stage. I responded "Josh and I have been working from 7:00am to 8:00pm every day and working every weekend". When Paul accepted his award my Regional Vice President said, "I just want to give a huge congratulations to Paul. He has been very instrumental in turning around the branch where Ross is filling in as the acting branch manager. No one from that branch has been an attendee at this event in over a year. Paul's work has gotten Ross, and Josh here at this event." The truth I told to Gerald about how the store got turned around now looked like a lie. How could my work be properly appreciated if someone else took credit for it? Not only was it taken credit for, but the person who took the credit for it told us not to tell anyone. Paul buried the truth and made us bury it even deeper by instructing us not to tell anyone. Paul had not spent an hour working at my branch but made it look like he went above and beyond at my branch.

Josh got promoted a week later. It was against Paul's initial plan for him to get promoted to another store but the fact that he was moving forward made me feel better after Paul took credit for our success. It's amazing what you can accomplish when you don't care about who gets the credit. As long as the pay checks made sense I didn't care if who took credit for it didn't make sense. When I began preparing for my next promotion by learning more about the bottom line, I realized that my pay checks didn't make sense. Our branch's profits had increased by 358%. Since turning the store around my area manager earned an average of $5,000 extra monthly. I averaged an extra $300 a month even though I was doing majority of the work to make the profits increase. The streets taught me to never be a pocket watcher, but when you are running a business you have to watch every pocket. You even have to pocket watch as an employee because you have to fairly assess your market value. Josh being recently promoted kept me with a tunnel vision to keep performing although the compensation I received for turning the store around was disrespectful.

When I got promoted to assistant manager I moved from my brother's house into an apartment by myself. Knowing I could get promoted again in a short timeframe I decided not to hook up my television or videogame system. I sacrificed anything that would distract me from bettering my craft during my free time. No vacations, no television, no partying, and no video games. After I finished in the top three several months in a row I figured it was perfect timing to take my first vacation since I had been with the company.

This was my second time being back in New Orleans since I changed my life. The dust finally settled with my enemies who remained on my mind while I was away. Shooter's killer had been sentenced to life in jail for second degree murder. Jake was jailed for a white collar crime, and Bianca got married then moved to Chicago. God had taken care of all my previous obstacles to make it out. Being home made me realize that I could prevail through anything. Within being home for one day I told over ten people about my journey in corporate America and what I accomplished at my current store. I also told them that I would be getting promoted to branch manager at my store real soon. Many times in life you are so busy working to accomplish your goals that you do not sit back and take heed of what you accomplished. Having my family and friends to help me realize what I had accomplished was one of the most rewarding memories of my management career.

I decided to check my work email after I woke up on my second day of vacation. Paul sent out an email opening up the branch manager position at my store. I was beyond excited until I read the qualifications to apply. The sentence that caused some concern was, "You must be a current branch manager to apply". I figured it had to be a mistake for a few reasons. He promised me that I would get promoted to branch manager if I turned the store around, and I did more than just turn it around. He had already broken one promise by promoting Josh elsewhere. Plus it would be poor logic to make a change in management when the current person at the helm took the branch from worst to first. I called Paul's cell phone for the next few days and he never returned my call. I spent the rest of my vacation stressed out. So much time had been spent away from my loved ones, and the time I spent with them I was stressed over what kept me away from them.

It was as if Paul waited for me to go on vacation to open up the position. Gerald called me on the drive back to Houston. He told me that he and the manager down the street were the

127

finalists for the position. The new manager down the street had only been with the company for two years and only won four trophies. Gerald had been with the company for ten years and had more than fifty trophies. My assumption that Gerald would get the position calmed me down a little bit. However my anger was far from gone because I was sold a dream that I wholeheartedly chased. Gerald did not sound as confident as I did that he would get the position. He felt he wouldn't get the position because Daniel and Paul golfed together. Daniel was also notoriously known as the biggest brownnose known to mankind.

My first Monday back I officially heard from Paul's mouth that I was not in the running for the branch manager position. Paul rarely came to my branch but he showed up to ask me what I thought about the candidates that he was considering for the spot. He rattled off a list of names that did not include mines. I was tickled pink that he acted as if he didn't have to address the promise he broke. I wanted to storm out like Josh did, except never come back. I couldn't help but stiffly ask him, "Why am I not a candidate for the spot? Better yet. Why am I not the favorite?" "There is a pecking order" Paul responded. "Where was the pecking order when I was the acting branch manager for the past few months? Also you told me if I turned the branch around I would get the position." I replied. Paul gathered his belongings and said, "You misunderstood me. Plus you weren't saying anything about it so I figured you weren't interested anymore. I have to go. We'll talk later." What Paul previously told me came full circle. Paul had previously told me, when it comes to getting promoted it's not about who the best performer is. It's about who has the right relationships and who has been in the decision maker's ear. Proving I was a top performer wasn't enough to solidify a promotion. It wasn't enough to earn Gerald the position either. Paul decided to go with Daniel instead of him.

Paul called me at the end of my shift on Monday and told me of his decision to go with Daniel as the new branch manager. I couldn't have been less concerned with talking about that. After Paul told me the news I asked, "What are your plans for me?" He responded, "I have plans for you. I will get you to my level one day. You are my star player, but I have to keep my clipboard close to my chest." I felt it in his voice that he didn't have any plans for me. I hate talking about real shit through text messages and over the phone because you can't look people in their eyes and read their body language. Those two things will tell you all you need to know. He dodged almost all of my questions, and did not elaborate on anything. That was the second time that he referred to my ceiling as his level. He did not share the mindset to make his employees better than him as I did. It was as if he thought I was not good enough to outdo his accomplishments.

Daniel getting promoted to my store opened up a new branch manager position in my area. Paul decided not to open up the new spot. He placed another assistant manager in the area as the acting branch manager in Daniel's previous position. Peter, the guy he chose as the acting branch manager was a friend of mines. He hated the company so much and had an exit plan that was already put into play. I was the only person who knew of his secret game plan. Not only did Paul overlook me again for a branch manager opportunity which was an insult to injury, he slighted someone else by not paying them appropriately for the work they performed. Peter was in the same situation I was in as far as that was concerned. Both of us were doing branch manager work but getting assistant manager pay. Paul's business mindset and integrity took a severe hit. I also began to question the company's hierarchy since promotions were based on relationships instead of performance.

Daniel had two weeks until his start date, and it was our replacement for Josh first day also. Danny was Josh's replacement. He was a different breed from a typical manager trainee with the company. Usually all of the employees at the entry level position were recent college graduates. Only a small percent of recent college grads have the responsibility and motivation to provide for a family. Also most recent college grads have yet to experience the trials and tribulations of corporate America. Danny was married and had three kids. He had also experienced the highs and lows of corporate America. His last job was a mid-senior level position at an oil and gas company. Danny was laid off during an oil and gas crisis. He was out of work for ten months and accepted the manager trainee position which he was overqualified for. He was sold on the opportunity to move up quick and learn how to run a business like I was. Danny spent every minute of his first two weeks by my hip. He shadowed everything I did, and asked the right questions. More ground was made by Danny in two weeks than most employees make in two months. He was already performing like a seasoned veteran. Danny had everything down pat in my system. I prayed that he would continue to perform at a high level once Daniel started.

The day before Daniel's start date moved by so slow because it was the last day running the business that I erected from the dumps. It's simple to lose sight that you have zero ownership in a company when you are a manager on the front lines making vital decisions on a daily basis. You are just a temporary owner. There is a limited amount of money you can make no matter how much money you generate the company. Danny was not aware that Daniel would be taking over the branch the next day, and neither were any of the customers. Tiffany and the rest of my employees who knew did not acknowledge the change that was about to take place. I did not bring it up to any customers, but I had to tell Danny. His response was, "Why when everything is going so perfect?" I did not have a legit answer for him because I couldn't even understand why. That day felt like a wake. The next day we were burying work as we once knew it.

Shit hit the fan as soon as the branch opened the next day. Usually when we got to the branch it was similar to a high school, in the aspect of although you saw the same people every day you embraced them with a handshake and a warm gesture as if you hadn't seen them since last summer. Everyone gave each other dry gestures and remained silent before we opened the branch. One of the most underrated values at work is morale. If employees are happy to come to work, and know their colleagues have their back that will correlate with positive results. If no one is happy to come to work, and there is no trust throughout the office, performance is guaranteed to trend downwards. Today was the funeral. We officially buried work as we once knew it. The vibe was dead. It was opening time at 7:30am and Daniel had still not arrived. The first customer must have felt the vibe because the first question he asked us was, "Did someone die in here?" I responded, "Something like that?" Daniel walked in the door simultaneously as I answered the customer's question. The customer looked at me and said, "It's going to be alright boss man." "Oh no. I am the new boss", Daniel butted in. The customer responded to Daniel, "The boss of what?" Daniel proudly responded, "The boss of this store. Ross is no longer in charge." The customer raised his eyebrows in a dismissive manner and said, "You sure don't act like a boss. Move along." The mood had been lightened. Everyone besides Daniel fell into laughter. Daniel continued on to his office and didn't speak to anyone on the way there. He remained in his office the entire morning and avoided helping during the busiest time of the day. Daniel finally came out of his office in the afternoon ten minutes before Paul arrived. It was amazing what impeccable timing Daniel had. "How did everything go this morning?" Paul asked Daniel. He responded, "We've been killing it." Everyone in the branch looked at each other as if everyone smelt someone pass gas at the same time when Daniel responded. Daniel had already proven to us he was full of shit twice.

Paul invited Daniel and I to lunch shortly after he arrived. I usually met Paul at the restaurant when we did lunch but we rode together this time. Before we could make it to our destination, the game was peeped. On the way to the restaurant Paul and Daniel aggressively picked my brain on how I turned the store around. In the past few years no manager had any success at the branch besides me. I began to get the hunch that I did not get promoted to Daniel's old branch so I could train my replacement. At that point I had been so alert to the games that were being ran in Corporate America so I decided not to fall victim to this one. But who would I be to pass up a free meal? Every time I had been to lunch with Paul our discussions were leisure based. This entire lunch I was bombarded with work related questions about running the branch. I bombarded back with rebuttals that it was just luck and it did not take much to make the branch successful. They pried and pried, and I lied and lied. At the end of the lunch they had the audacity to appear aggravated that I did not give them any valuable game. Why was I being asked these questions if Daniel were a better fit than me to be the branch manager and if Paul was the reason for the store's recent success?

I decided to remain professional and not give in to the hostile environment. I continued to perform every day and smile during every interaction with Daniel so he could never fix his mouth to say anything negative about me. He couldn't belittle me as he tried to do on my first day because of my experience at the oil and gas company. Daniel tried to entice me several times to respond negatively towards his mental games but I had been well prepared from dealing with Roger and Todd. It burned him up that there was nothing he could do to negatively affect my performance or my positive mood. He decided to exert his negative energy on everyone else in the branch. Within one month he had accused Tiffany of stealing twice when he actually misplaced what he had accused her of stealing. Also he attempted to belittle Danny several times and teased our mentally challenged porter in front of customers twice. At the end of Daniel's first month it was no surprise that we plummeted from 2nd place in the region to 18th place. I was surprised we didn't drop further in the rankings.

I was in the same situation that Josh was in at the beginning of his career. My previous month was a waste. I did not finish in the top 1/3rd because of numbers that I did not have full control of. This was the first time I did not finish in the top 33% since being with the company. Having groundbreaking accomplishments would be irrelevant if I didn't finish in the top 33% the next two months. It seemed impossible to finish any higher going forward because I finished first in every individual category and my store was in a drastic down spiral. Everyone in the branch was stressed out because of new management. The vibe was extremely toxic. It would be harder than before to turn the store back around. I decided to invite Paul to lunch. It was my first time ever inviting someone who managed me to lunch. It was urgent that I got answers and found a way out of this situation that was headed nowhere fast. If I didn't, all the hard work I put in would go to waste. Paul was back to only talking about leisure once we sat down at lunch. I was intrigued that he did not take a businesslike approach with our interactions during lunch as he did with Daniel. It seemed as if he had no plans on moving me forward and I had to get aggressive on figuring that out.

The first question Paul asked when we were seated at the table was, "What are you doing this weekend?" I responded, "I don't know. What's next for me Paul?" He didn't have that answer planned out yet. So he replied, "You tell me." "You hired Daniel to do what I thought was planned for me.", I responded. In the most nonchalant manner Paul replied, "Why didn't you say anything? I thought you didn't want it because you never bought it up to me. Daniel spoke about it every week to me, so I figured that he wanted it the most. What's next for you is to help Daniel get the store up and running like you had it." It was evident that Paul would be resilient with his mind games. If persuading him with my performance wasn't enough, then I don't think persuading him at lunch would help much either. It was time to get straight to the point, because staying at the store with Daniel was not an option. I looked at Paul and said, "I have proven that I am ready to be a branch manager and if I am not allowed that opportunity here, then I will be forced to look outside of your area for a promotion." Paul responded, "You have done so much for the area. I can't let you go just like that." Paul's response made it seem like I was at work for him instead of the company. Prior to having lunch with Paul I felt like he had the upper hand going forward. After lunch I felt like he exposed his hand and that gave me the upper hand. If the store were to fail after he hired Daniel instead of me then his poor decision making would be exposed. After we finished lunch and it was time to part ways Paul asked me to give him some time and he would take care of me.

I had finally pulled up to the fork in the road. Month two of Daniel's tenure as my manager had finally came to an end. The final rankings were nothing to be optimistic about. During Daniel's second month he racially profiled three minority customers, did nothing to positively impact the branch's bottom line, and provoked an argument with Danny that almost came to blows. My production increased with my sense of urgency to get promoted out of the store. Peter called me at 6:30am on the morning we received our final rankings. He usually only called me during the day to tell me jokes about how much he hated the company. I guess he had a really funny one if he was calling me at 6:30am in the morning. As soon as I picked up the phone Peter said, "Hey Ross, I am quitting man. You can have this branch. I got hired at the company that I have been trying to get on at for over two years. I don't see why he didn't give you this store in the first place." I responded, "Congrats my brother. I am happy for you. I probably still won't get the spot though." Peter ended our conversation by saying "Don't worry if you don't bro. You deserve better than this company. Call me after your lunch. I have something else that will make you laugh besides this." There was no need to stop for coffee after that call.

Peter's phone call was great news. I love seeing my friends succeed, but it didn't change the fact that I wasn't looking forward to seeing the final rankings. I couldn't believe how much of a sunken place I had fell mentally. I was anticipating having a bad day. The rankings were in my email waiting on me. I finished close to last place overall in the standings but I finished top three in every individual statistic. The store numbers took an even bigger drop to no surprise of mines. My branch had the worst customer service score in the region. It gave me great pleasure to watch Daniel and Paul read the final rankings. Daniel and Paul's actions of panic balanced out the anger I had built inside. It was enjoyable to watch them stress over the store's downfall. There was no reason for me to be sympathetic for them failing at their crooked plan, but it was out of my character to laugh at other's failures. That was the first time I laughed at someone else's downfall since elementary school. Corporate America got me to go against my life values again.

Paul's decision making skills and Daniel's managing skills were on full display. This gave me the upper hand that I lusted for. I held back my laugh for about thirty minutes as Daniel and Paul sat at the branch in distress. After an hour I finally figured out what Peter was talking about when he said, he had something else that was funny. He quit, but not only did he quit. He gave a one day notice instead of a two week notice. Most employers request for a two week notice of resignation to give them ample time to fill the person's position who resigned. Having twenty-four hours to find a replacement to run a million dollar plus operation is quite an urgent situation. I had the luxury of watching Paul receive the news. His plan to underpay someone for a branch manager role for as long as he could again came to a halt when Peter resigned immediately. Paul ran out of the store, and sped off to attempt to convince him to stay longer than a day. Peter did not budge on staying longer than that day.

Paul called Daniel and asked him to inform me of my interview for the vacant position later that same evening. After all of the work I put in, my promotion was no moment of glory. It was given to me out of last resort instead of being awarded to me as I deserved. My promotions in the streets felt more rewarding than this promotion. The extra $15,000 annually from my promotion did not compensate for the pain I went through to get it. I knew my promotion would generate me more money than I ever had but the things I had to endure to make that money were mentally taxing me. It caused me to go to the lowest and darkest places. Each step became progressively more stressful, and embarking on this new step I knew things would become more stressful than I could imagine. Knowing that soured the day I had been anticipating for the prior three hundred and sixty-five days. During my interview with Paul he had the nerve to act as if I wasn't a shoe in for the position. He also acted as if he were gambling on me if he decided to choose me for the position. It was like he was dangling a tennis ball in front of a dog who he crippled. Paul talked about business the entire conversation for the first time ever. It was odd that he asked me similar questions from the day he did when he took me and Daniel to lunch. He may have seen this as his best, and last opportunity to help Daniel. I gave him a little knowledge to get by in the interview but I kept a lot in my back pocket due to the disrespect of my intelligence.

Chapter 15

Becoming a branch manager was the reason why I got out of bed every morning for the past year with the rental car company, and it was also the reason why I took the job. I was officially "running a business" as the company likes to call it. I had the experience of "running a business" by their lingo before I had the official title. If turning around a negatively profiting store to one of the most profitable stores in the region was not enough to be treated with some respect then what would make them treat me with the respect I deserved? This was the lowest level of intensity and motivation I had entering any position. I knew I had the skillset to kill it, but knowing what I was compensated with for killing it last time deterred my motivation. All of those trophies were useless. Before my first day at my new position I sat down with Gerald to better understand the bottom line and my new pay structure. I calculated that I was well on target to make $60,000 a year going forward. The initial number sounded like a decent amount until I read that I would be making the company over $15,000,000 that year.

My first day was a culture shock. It was just like opening up a business from scratch. Nothing was established at this branch yet. No repeat customers, no reviews online, and I also did not have a sign in the front of my store. We were inside of an auto-mechanic shop that sat back two hundred feet from the street in the suburbs of Houston. The only signage that represented the company to potential customers who passed our branch was a bumper sticker sized sign in a window that was partially covered by bushes. Needless to say, not many people knew we were there. Not even every branch manager in my area knew where my new store was located. My new branch was opened within the past year. It is harder to turn a brand new store to a high performing one than turning around a low performing store. Managing an established business means you have preexisting analytics and you have opportunities to see what adjustments can be made to the current flow of business. Also no culture was set. Everything was on me to establish a culture and to bring new customers in.

During my first few months at the helm my store averaged three customers a day. Scott was the only manager trainee I had at my new store. He was similar to Danny in the regard of his age and work ethic, but very different in skillset. He was twenty years into his professional career and this was his first sales position. Every challenge this store presented to me were new ones. This was the opportunity to build a store from scratch and stamp my brand on it. My other colleague's name was Lucas. His position was the branch's porter. He was socially and mentally challenged, but he knew a lot about electronics and technology. On my first day while I sat at my computer he reached by my feet to pick up a piece of trash and unnecessarily gently placed his left hand on my back then smiled at me. After he picked up the trash he asked, "You don't mind if I touch you like that right?" "Not if you want to keep your teeth." I replied. The appropriate thing to do would have been to report him to Human Resources, but I had an overzealous heart for people with social and mental conditions. This was an opportunity to show him that he could trust me. We only had fifty vehicles in our entire fleet at my new location. That was one fourth of the amount of cars that I had at my old store. My promotion felt like a demotion because of the lack of responsibilities I had compared to my previous position. It was as if I was dropped from the professionals to junior varsity.

Regardless of me previously having success at managing a higher volume store, I struggled to perform my first few months at my new position. Lucas struggled with the simplest of tasks such as remembering to pick someone up right after being reminded to and poorly cleaning cars that we had to rent to customers. We had to rewash almost every car that he claimed he was finished cleaning. He was detrimental to our customer service scores. No matter how nice and professional Scott and I could be it was nullified if a customer was picked up late and their car was given to them dirty. Scott had done great with customer service, marketing, and professionalism but he still struggled to catch on regarding sales. Because Scott was a manager trainee his main job responsibility was to take a bulk of the sales. The lack of sales was detrimental to our operating profit. My paycheck was also slimmer than my previous ones as an acting branch manager. I wondered why Paul did not take me and Daniel to lunch again to ask him questions in my benefit. Let alone why he had been missing in action for my entire tenure so far at this new position.

Once I had a few months to see what I had been doing wrong, and doing right it motivated me to see how effective my adjustments would be. Seeing my name on the bottom of the overall rankings activated my pride. Having a point to prove, and Josh getting promoted to a branch manager position made me enjoy my job again. During my fourth month I finally figured out my groove. Scott had become a top seller throughout the region and we had grown our fleet to a hundred cars. The summer could not have come at a better time. We bought on two porters for the summer for temporary work. Lucas's deficiencies were able to be hidden with the additional help. After doubling our fleet size the help was badly needed. We achieved an above average customer service score and I was back performing at a high level. A customer service score was the most important metric for a branch manager. If your customer service score is not above corporate average you are not eligible for a promotion.

By the time summer ended, we had 130 cars in the fleet and I finally moved back to the top of the rankings. Usually rental car stores drop off in volume during the fall, but our volume of business continued to increase. Customers had a unique experience when they came to rent from my store. I decided to go with a diverse marketing approach. We turned customers who came in to rent because of car malfunction into renters for leisure purposes, grew our corporate business, and drove in new personal use renters. Our explosive growth increased our profits but our customer service scores decreased below corporate average because Lucas's deficiencies could no longer be hidden with the temporary porters gone.

Before the end of fall I grew my business three times of its initial size from when I first started. Unfortunately I still had the same amount of employees I had when I first started. It was not nearly enough man power to handle the increased volume. Paul was back having the upper hand. It would not have benefited him much to give me the extra employees that I desperately needed. The most important metric for an area manager was their customer service score also. However their customer service score is calculated different from branch managers. An area manager has at least nine stores in their area. Therefore the size of the store influences the weight of impact each store has on the area manager's customer service score. Because my store was the newest one in the area and every other store in my area had been open for over seven years my store was the smallest in size. Consequently my store had the smallest impact on Paul's customer service score. If I had a 99 out of 100 or a 65 it wouldn't make a big difference regarding my manager's promotability, but it meant the world to my promotability. Paul took full advantage of the situation and repeatedly denied me of hiring a new employee. I had already proven I could flourish while being short staffed, so he made me do it again. To counteract being short staffed, I worked seventy plus hours a week, every weekend, and spent majority of my scarce leisure time working.

My entire career Paul tricked me into keeping the things I did that were above and beyond between me and him. There was no way my accomplishments would be appropriately appreciated and respected if others did not know what I went through to earn them. Only a few people in the entire company knew the depths I went to be successful. Throughout the company people acted is if my accomplishments were handed to me and I was expected to finish at the top every month with ease. It reminded me of the sports player who continued to finish on top and the fans had no clue about the amount of work they put in after practice and the off-season to make it to their level of excellence. I was kept at bay by Paul continuously complementing me but his compliments came with no significant rewards. A $20 gift card and a, "Hey, you are killing it." was a disrespectful compensation. Most importantly, I learned nothing from Paul also. Every time I asked him for business advice, or about company knowledge he would give me answers that would be of no help. It was as if he were playing dumb, but maybe he wasn't playing.

By the milestone of my two year anniversary with the company, I earned two promotions in record time and developed four employees that earned managerial promotions. That along with several other amazing accomplishments gave me the ambition to work until retirement age at the rental car company. I was already legendary despite the fact that I was fairly new with the company. I imagined what I could get accomplished in the upcoming years with the company. It felt as if it were January 1st mentally, but I was quickly reminded that it was closer to July 1st by the thunderous storm outside. That was a day you knew the sun would not come out. It seemed as if it were raining everywhere in the world. Most people see times like that as a time to relax. I saw times like that as a perfect time to go harder because I knew most of my competitors were relaxing. My mind was flooding simultaneously as the rain water flooded the streets. The storm continued the entire week consequently we only had five customers in five days. Prior to that we were averaging five customers by 9:00am every morning. I thought I moved away from the flooding but evidently it flooded here also. That was a historic storm in Houston, Texas. Lives, houses, buildings, and vehicles were lost in the storm. It was a tragic event that I was all too familiar with. Unless you have been through a catastrophe such as a hurricane, earthquake, tornado etc., there is no other way to know what those experiences were like. Because of so, I had an extra sympathetic heart for those affected by the storm.

The need for rental cars greatly surpassed what was originally projected by the corporate office. That Saturday I had over twenty potential customers whose cars were damaged from the storm waiting outside of my branch before opening time. Lucas and I were the only people at work. Each Saturday I was only allowed to have one person working with me. On Saturdays every store in the region closed at 12:00pm. When the clock struck 11:00am, my office still had over fifteen customers in the lobby wanting to do business. Lucas said he was too stressed out, so he left at 12:00pm. Every branch in the region decided to shut down at 12:00pm also, but I decided to keep my branch open until 6:00pm. I continued to have that dogmatic hustle the entire month and grew my store by an extra fifty cars. The company's expectation was for each branch manager to grow their store by 10% of previous year to date fleet size. Every month I was above 50% but now I was over 100%. Those efforts still didn't land me the customer service scores I needed to get promoted. Barely any phone calls were answered, customers were almost always picked up and dropped off late, and I was barely able to make any follow up calls with customers to verify that they had no problems with their rental experience. I was set up to fail. The main agenda pushed by my higher ups was to grow your store as much as possible but my growth was not supported. My income was good, but it could have been great. I was subject to make that income because I was not eligible to get promoted which would earn me even more money.

I decided to go against my own principles again and reach out to HR. It is very important to keep a paper trail on important conversations in Corporate America. Creating a paper trail preferably by email is the best way to hold the other party of the dialog accountable for what they said and can always be used as a point of reference. Someone can tell you anything on the phone or in person but if the situation is revisited then it will be your word against theirs. Paul had not written me up yet for my customer service scores, but I knew I was at risk to be documented. When I involved Human Resources I magically received a second manager trainee and two new porters. It felt unreal to have a third body in the branch to help handle phone calls, sales, and marketing. Before then I did not feel like a manager. I was the marketing department, sales department, head porter, and the customer service team. A typical work day would involve me starting my day by washing cars before opening the branch. Then making sales in a fast paced environment during the morning rush and handling customer service issues. After that I would go marketing, and shove some lunch in my face while driving back to the branch. When I arrived back to the branch I would repeat my morning schedule until an hour after closing time. It felt like a luxury to finally do the job description of my own instead of three other positions and their job duties.

After my first month of working with our new staff I achieved a customer service score well above corporate average. Danny also got promoted to branch manager. Josh and Danny's success felt better than any individual feat I accomplished. My development skills were unmatched. No one else had developed two branch managers in less than two and a half years of being with the company. I also received the best possible news I could ever receive in life. My first child was on the way. That was by far the most rewarding feeling ever. Knowing I would be a father gave me the ultimate motivation to become the epitome of a man and to be successful for my child. I felt as though my seed was watching my moves every step of the way without physically being present. One thing that Paul and I had in common was our love for family. He had five children and I always wanted five children. Wanting that many kids is a rarity amongst millennials. Our mutual love for big families was what kept our bond from breaking when it was on thin ice. Paul invited me to lunch once I gave him the amazing news about the new edition to my family. He was the first person I told that I had a child on the way after my parents. We had some tough times but I still felt we were that close to tell him second. Informing him second deepened our bond. Paul gave me a great motivational speech while we were at lunch that motivated me to take my hustle to new depths. "The responsibility of heading a household will have you working through obstacles that you deemed unimaginable, but that is deemed necessary to provide", is what he left me with as we finished lunch and went our separate ways.

Who knew what he was talking about would come full circle in a few months. Paul promoted my new manager trainee that HR sent me when a new assistant manager position opened in the area. I was back at square one with personnel. My staff consisted of Ralph, who was a brand new manager trainee that graduated from college a few weeks before he was hired and Lucas. Ralph was well polished, hungry, and gifted. One of the most important factors in life that isn't respected enough is timing. Not one branch manager position opened during the months when I was promotable. I earned a high customer service score every month after HR sent me some more employees. It was obvious that I could achieve above corporate average customer service scores when I wasn't extremely short staffed. I was now the head of the household, and this was my only option available to be able to provide for my family with that type of income. I would be up against the unimaginable going forward, but it was necessary. I couldn't believe Paul would use that against me to hold my career back.

My experiences in life taught me that it's not about the hand you are dealt. It's about how you play the hand you are dealt. To compensate for the loss of the promoted manager trainee, Paul sent me a senior citizen driver who was barely physically active. I only had one spade in my hand, and that was Ralph. I needed to get Lucas up to par. So I decided to have my seventieth heart to heart with him. Long walks around the branch and talks on long drives weren't getting through to Lucas to get him to improve. Paul had been trying to get me to terminate Lucas since the beginning of my tenure, but I stood up for him as if he were my own blood. That's the only reason he was still employed with the company. Lucas always had a new person to complain about every day, whether it was someone off of a social media site, an employee, or even a customer. You have to know that if someone talks about other people behind their back consistently there is a high probability that you could be next. I found out I was next that following morning. Several customers and one employee approached me before lunch time to inform me that Lucas had been negatively talking about me behind my back. Usually once someone does me wrong I don't try to figure out why. I just move on and let their conscience eat them up, but I couldn't let this slide without knowing why. I had already planned to take him to lunch to see what I could do to help him improve, but now time was taking away from that because I had to figure out why the disrespect was taking place behind my back. When Lucas sat down across from me at lunch he had the look of a child who was preparing themselves for a whipping. During the lunch I concluded that he was not mentally competent to do what was required of him as an employee. He lied to me about everything even if it wasn't work related. Also he couldn't rebuttal anything sensible about plans to improve his poor work performance.

For the next five months I lived every minute as if my son was watching me. I gave my maximum effort every day. Every morning besides Sunday I was up before sunrise. I treated every day with a sense of urgency and I did not stop working at night until my body gave out. That resulted in making more money than what I was projected to, but I still fell short of the customer service scores I needed to get promoted because I did not have adequate staffing. The call finally came that I had been anticipating. My baby boy was on the way.

While I was doing a few last minute tasks before I left for paternity leave it struck me that every time I left to go back home for a check up on my son over twenty vehicles were missing out of our fleet. Losing vehicles is losing money so I had Ralph to make note of the cars that we lost and gained everyday while I was gone. After I finished packing up my things to head to the hospital I was stopped in my tracks by a reflection. It was my own reflection in the mirror that was unrecognizable. I had gained over thirty pounds, and was drained from stress. My experiences in Corporate America aged me at an accelerated rate.

Chapter 16

While I was away for paternity leave, my phone rang consistently. My phone even rang while my son was being born. I had ignored almost every call and text while I was away for my son's birth, but work was still not free from my mind during the most important time of my life. I had initially planned to stay on leave for a week after my son's birth, but I had to leave the day after my son was born because Ralph got sick and Paul said he couldn't find another replacement to run my store. One day, or even one decision at my branch could destroy my month financially. So anytime I was not there, I had to keep my branch on my mind. My mind couldn't even be freed from work during my lunch breaks, let alone be freed while I was on leave for a week. I had no choice but to cut my trip short and head back to work.

The time I had been working for my entire life was now here. You learn so much about yourself when something you previously asked for finally presents itself. You will see if you are prepared for what you asked for and see what levels you will go to succeed at the opportunity you requested. I had my entire family on my back that I was responsible for now. Everything that I asked for was now a daily responsibility of mines until the end of time.

When Ralph arrived back at work he told me Paul had given away thirty of my cars to other branches although we still had customers who wanted to rent them. I had an even worse taste in my mouth than what he did the last time I went on vacation. I did not address Paul about it. I still had tunnel vision from my child's birth and did not want to deal with anything that could alter my happiness. My child's mother had to wait two months before her and my son could move to Texas. Those two months felt like an eternity. I had missed the first two months of my son's life because of work. My purpose of going to college was to get a great paying job, and I finally had one but it was not fulfilling to me as I assumed it would be. My freedom to enjoy life was restricted. Happiness was a distant memory. My stress levels were at an all-time high, and I missed priceless moments that I could never get back. I was entrapped because I did not have another option where I could make the amount of money I made immediately and I was already going through a major transition in life that did not have any space for another one.

The Monday before my family moved to Texas, Paul gave me my first write up. The documentation could not have come at a better time. My family moving with me that week shielded me with happiness. If I would have been administered a write up during any other time I would have lost my mind. I was numb to anything negative because of the birth of my son. That write up did something to my soul knowing that my way of living could be taken away from me at any moment by another person regardless if they were right or wrong. That was exactly what I needed to take me to new heights. I became invincible for the next several months after that day. I could do no wrong and had worked my way back to prominence in the company. I put up numbers that were never seen before again. Nothing changed in our cycle of service. Customers finally came to the conclusion that we were trying our absolute best and we did not have enough manpower to service the amount of customers we had. The sympathy from my customers gave me an awareness of what I was going through, and I could no longer turn a blind eye to what I had endured. I decided it was perfect timing to revisit the conversation with my manager about moving forward with the company. So I invited him to lunch.

Before the waitress could bring us a cup of water I asked

147

Paul, "What his plans were for me moving forward?" He responded, "For you to maintain your customer service score for another year." "Another year? I qualify to get promoted right now and I have consistently been a top performer even without being provided the adequate help to get the job done. I can't continue working seventy plus hours a week and killing myself like this. Plus I just placed top 10 out of three regions." I said in a defeated voice. "Yes, but that's what I need to see before I let you get promoted." he responded. It was so entertaining that he wanted to see more from me to get promoted when countless of other people who didn't have one third of the credentials as me got promoted since I had been in the same position. "I am ready to move to the next level." I responded. He concluded the discussion by saying, "You made $70,000 a year at twenty-five years old. You need to maintain that level before you take on too much. He made it clear that he felt I was not supposed to surpass the level I was at financially because of my age and other obvious reasons.

Josh and Danny were both fired for extremely poor reasons. Danny fell victim to a he said she said situation that involved a well-known liar. Paul attempted to get Josh fired five times and it worked on the sixth time. It was obvious that Paul was motivated by other reasons than protecting company policy. It was no other way to see it than Paul fired them for ulterior motives. It was heartbreaking to watch two men who were the breadwinners for their families making over $70,000 a year get fired for unjustifiable reasons. After Paul fired Danny and Josh he suggested that I should end my friendship with them. It was one of the most distasteful things that was ever told to me. Word got out that Paul was asked to take a pay cut from his higher ups. He decided to lower his expenses throughout the area instead. Danny and Josh were extremely talented and ethical employees that fell victims to a salary sweep. Both made over $20,000 a year than what they were originally projected to make. Therefore Paul made an extra $90,000. Paul's paycheck is an expense that comes out of his manager's salary. Just like how my paycheck comes out of his salary. Paul saw Josh and Danny's salary as an opportunity to lower expenses and save himself. I no longer felt safe because I also made way more than what I was projected to make.

A "middle class" is one of the biggest allusions and revolving doors in the United States. Technically I was a member of the middle class during that time period. If I were to be fired or laid off I had nothing to fall back on and I would quickly be a part of the lower class again. My family owned no assets, well vested stock, paid off housing, land, and could not provide me with residual income. All I had was money in a bank account and money saved that I would be heavily taxed on if I touched it before a certain age although it was my money. Also $70,000 jobs weren't floating around in society.

I decided to keep a low profile for the next few months so I could slide under the radar. I also cut back on the amount of business I took in so I could make it easier to achieve higher customer service scores and to lower profits. I actually tried to make less money. Corporate America put me in the situation to do the dumbest thing possible.

My career at the company was not the only thing that I had put everything into, and was on the verge of losing. My child's mother threatened to move from Houston because I spent all of my time working or stressing about work. The little time I had for my family I was of no use. I would fall asleep during anytime we tried to do something and when I was awake I mainly talked about work. Not only did I not have time for them, I had no time for the rest of my family, or friends. I didn't even have time for myself. I would get up at 4:30am to work out several times a week because that was the only time I could make it to the gym. Then leave for work at 6:30am, and arrive back home at 7:30pm. I repeated that grueling process five days out of the week. On Saturday I would work from 7:00am to 3:00pm. I was too burnt out from the work week to do anything until Monday morning. I didn't even want to live with myself, so I couldn't blame someone else for not wanting to live with me.

I was backed into a corner that I knew only God could get me out of. I asked God for a sign on what I needed to do and prayed myself to sleep. I went to sleep stressed and woke up blessed. It felt like all my problems had left my mind and I was rejuvenated. When I pulled up to work thirty minutes early there was a guy sitting on the bench in the front of my branch. He had a New Orleans Saints hat on. That was an easy icebreaker. I walked up to him and said, "Good morning sir. How could I help you?" Normally I would have went through the back door to sneak in so a customer could not see me come in early. I don't know if it was intuition or because he had on a hat representing my home city. He responded in a pressed manner, "I have to ride with my boss to pick up his nephew from New Orleans today, and it's urgent that we get there ASAP." I decided to take him in ten minutes before my store opened. He looked very familiar, but I could not figure out where I knew him from. Most people who knew me from New Orleans who hadn't seen me in a while had a hard time recognizing me. I had gained more than forty pounds, cut all of my facial hair off, and changed my way of living. I did not go the extra mile to figure out where I knew him from because I know whenever I met him back home that I was not that same person anymore. After he told me what he did for a living and where he hung out at my hunch that I knew him got even stronger. As I prepared his transaction I saw him in my peripheral vision watching me the entire time he sat in the waiting area. After we finished our transaction he said, "Thank you. I owe you one."

I had some exciting news waiting for me in my email. A branch manager spot opened up in another region. The hiring area manager was a black man who I had dreamed of working for since I began with the company. The store with a vacant branch manager position was only slightly larger than my store but change was long overdue. I had been to hell and back with Paul, but I still felt sad about having to tell him that I intended to leave the area. The intake of customers was light that morning so I had time to put my ear to the streets to see who else was applying for the position. One good thing I loved about the company was that external candidates had to start at the manager trainee position. I was one of the only elite branch managers without a flagship location. Five other managers put in for the open branch manager position also but if you combined all of their résumés it still wouldn't be half of mines. After finding out that there was a mutual interest with the hiring manager I began to celebrate.

The feeling of finally being able to earn close to a six figure salary after I had been through so much in Corporate America, and life bought me to tears. The timing couldn't have been better to have a scheduled half day off. I had to turn my phone off so I could give this special time in life my undivided attention. One of the biggest stressors in my life was the telephone. While I was away from work, customers would call me during the wee hours of the morning, and club hours at night. The work phone never stopped ringing and it usually rang until the voicemail picked up because we were rarely able to get to it due to how busy we were. Almost every five minutes for two years straight a phone rang or some type of alert was coming through my phone. I just wanted to toss that bitch in the Pacific Ocean, then take it out and throw it to the Atlantic Ocean. I felt like I was on an exotic vacation when I turned my cell phone off. Time finally slowed down. The rest of my day felt like a week. I took my entire family out to dinner so we could celebrate and catch up. After sitting at the dinner table with my family, my mother bought to my attention that I forgot about my niece's birthday, missed my uncle's funeral, and didn't attend two family weddings. All of those events were extremely important to me and I missed them because of corporate America. Around the people I love the most I felt in complete isolation and embarrassment.

Many people look at prison as modern day slavery. They have

to be told when to get up, eat, what to wear, how they can style themselves, and when they can be free. All of those things are being told to employees in corporate America. They have a certain time to be at work, a certain attire to wear, a certain time to eat lunch, and they are told which days they can be free. One may be quick to say you get paid more in corporate America than slavery. Yes you do, but just as slavery you are financially dependent on another person if you don't have other streams of income. If you don't have other streams of income outside of your employer then someone else will ultimately have control of your finances and way of living. My high about the position was slightly blown when I realized the only thing that would be changing in my life with the new position were my finances. I would still be subject to the same lifestyle, which was one I began to dread more than ever. The news of more money was not what my family wanted. My family wanted more time. Not having real money my entire life growing up put me into a tunnel vision of going through anything to get it. My family's expression of reluctance and concern still did not diminish my want for the promotion. I figured they would understand my sacrifices once I started making six figures.

The hiring area manager reached out to me on Wednesday and scheduled my interview for the following Tuesday. I had achieved everything there was to accomplish at my current store. I received awards for profit growth, customer service, fleet growth, and operating profit. I also developed over seven employees that received managerial promotions within the company. Because of that I mentally checked out and began to prepare for what was next with the company. Paul was out of town for that week so I had another reason to focus on things outside of my branch. I was the acting area manager while Paul was on vacation. I dedicated my time to mainly preparing for my interview and helping other branches in my area. On Friday morning I decided to take a look at the numbers of the week I was running the area. The numbers were up from previous weeks, and also my colleagues expressed how much more they enjoyed working versus typical weeks. It sucked that my growth was being limited by other people's opinion and I wasn't allowed to grow simultaneously with my actual development.

That Friday as I was preparing to go to lunch the customer who had the New Orleans Saints hat on was pulling into my branch's parking lot. I decided to push my lunch break back to complete his return. Fifteen minutes later he stood outside of the front door and called me to come outside. "I have someone who wants to talk to you in the car.", the customer whispered as I walked across the threshold. As I approached the car I did not know what to expect. With the car facing the opposite way it gave me even more of an anticipation because I could not see who was in the vehicle. When I crossed the trunk, the passenger side door opened. The car raised up as the oversized man got out of his seat. It was Derrick! It felt like seeing a ghost until he gave me a bear hug. Derrick stared at me for about five seconds and said, "I just got out. Jake tried to frame me for killing Uriah because we didn't want to bring him in on some business. I am done with that life. I had my boy Jimmy to track you down. I can't believe you changed your life like this. I am trying to do the same. Let's meet up Monday. I want to link you up with someone. See you then." Derrick got back in the car in a rushed manner then the person driving the car pulled off.

No matter where you go in life people will always find you. Hiding from something is not a logical way to live your life. Derrick's freedom was great. I was not sure if his presence was. I still owed him money from before he went to jail. Maybe he had bad motives to meet up with me, but no bad vibes were felt therefore I was excited to meet up with him. When I got back inside the branch Ralph and several other customers who were in the office asked me did I just find out I was having another baby. I carried on with that same glow until I got back from lunch. While I was in the back wash bay cleaning cars, I saw police officers pull into the parking lot then enter the front door of the branch.

My first instinct was to run, but I almost forgot that I was a law abiding citizen now. I did nothing to warrant an arrest. Nate, the manager of the auto-shop called my cell phone and told me, "Make your way to the front. The authorities want to speak to you." When I made it back to the front the police pulled me into my office. I tried to forget everything I saw before I went to lunch so I could best avoid the questions they were about to ask me. I assumed they were there to ask about Derrick.

A tall white officer with a crew cut was the first person to speak once we entered the office, "Do you know a guy by the name of Lucas who happens to work here?" "Yes I do.", I quickly responded. A shorter white cop asked the second question, "How well do you know him?" It took me a few seconds to answer the next question. I had just come to the realization that I was being cross examined about Lucas. "I know him professionally but that's it." I responded. The tall white officer asked, "Do you know him well enough to know that he wouldn't steal from a customer or colleague?" I responded, "I can't put nothing past anyone, and I have no knowledge of anything pertaining to these questions so I would be of no beneficial use to questions of this nature." Both of the investigators moved towards the office door and the taller one said, "FYI, to protect your business we have to inform you that we have proof of him being involved with theft from customers and employees. Please do not say anything because that will disrupt our investigation". They exited the premises after they left out of the office.

I had to get to the bottom of that immediately. It seemed that I was quite close to the bottom of it being that Ralph and another customer recently told me they had some weird activities in their bank account. Lucas was missing while the police were looking for him but he reappeared conveniently after the police pulled out of the parking lot. As I approached him another situation had deemed itself more urgent.

Ralph and Nate began to go back and forth about a brand new sports car that was just delivered to us before the cops came. Nate always wanted something for a little of nothing when it came to renting cars no matter the circumstance. Ralph had just got in trouble with Paul for renting Nate a luxury car for dirt cheap. Every time Nate asked Ralph for a car he would respond yes immediately. That evening was a little different. When Nate asked Ralph to reserve him the sports car Ralph responded, "I am going to have to let you know later". Nate became irritable when Ralph was reluctant to commit to the deal. I pulled Ralph outside away from the conversation to avoid it going further south. As soon as we got outside he said, "I have a repeat customer that's coming in for that car before we close and Nate is trying to pay $11 a day for it. What should I do?" If you make every decision for your employees, you will limit their growth. Their decision making skills will be dependent on others and will become tentative during time sensitive moments. You have to give your employees opportunities to make decisions as long as it isn't detrimental or irreparable to your business. "It's up to you." I responded. Ralph's face said it all, and he headed to the wash bay. Lucas was in the back office crying but I had to pretend like I didn't see him. I carried on handling the front office for thirty minutes, and in came the repeat customer who was interested in the sports car.

Before I could ask the customer how her day was going Ralph pulled up by the front door with the car she wanted. She pulled off in the car ten minutes later. The end of the business day couldn't have come at a better time. I bought Ralph his keys outside so he could avoid an argument with Nate. While I was walking back in and closing up the branch I overheard Lucas making excuses about the crimes he committed. I was not looking forward to working with him the next day.

To no surprise, Lucas decided to call off the following day. I was in for the grind by myself. Since almost all of my cars had got delivered the previous day and were brand new, I was free of my normal responsibility of cleaning cars on Saturday morning. I still showed up to work an hour early because my mind was so clouded from the previous day that I forgot it wasn't necessary to wash cars before the branch opened. When I arrived to work Nate wasted thirty minutes of my precious time fussing about what happened with him and Ralph. The phone began to ring as soon as I noticed he wasn't about to shut up anytime soon. I was never as happy to answer a phone call before business hours until that moment. I ran to the phone to pick up the call. The customer on the phone requested that I do him a favor that could get me fired. He asked the same question five different ways and I told him no five different times. He hung up the phone after he told me, "He was going to pull up on me." After two hours of simultaneously answering phone calls, washing cars, and completing transactions he came through on his word and pulled up on me.

A guy about six feet four inches tall stormed to the counter with two other men behind him. The tall guy who stormed to the front counter had to be the same guy that was on the phone. When he got to the counter he spoke over the customer who I was helping, and demanded that I do what he was asking me to do on the phone. I responded, "We are going around in a revolving door with this conversation. We can't keep doing this." The tough guy responded, "Look muthafucka! You don't have to talk to me like that! You are going to make me do you something! I am going to pull back up on you when you get off and show you what's up!" In a non-bothered manner I responded, "I am off right now. Do you want to go to the back right now and do something?" My response caused him to freeze up and resemble a deer in headlights. His friends made fun of him for cowering up and they left right after. It's amazing how customers of poor character disrespect people in the service industry. Many people who do so feel they can let their pre-consumed stress out on someone servicing them and can get away with it. 98% of those people would not talk to a random stranger the way they talk to someone servicing them at a place of business. The other 2% are menaces to society. I was thankful to be able to close up shop at the normally scheduled time that Saturday.

While I was locking up the branch, I received a text from Paul. I figured he texted me to applaud me for the great numbers that were put up while I was acting area manager. I was glad that he texted me because I was not ready to tell him that I found a position outside of the area. I opened the message, as soon as I turned the key to lock the door of the branch. The message was a long one. He must have found out about Lucas. I decided not to read it until I sat down in the car.

The message read, "Hey Ross, I got a call from Damon Stewart an area manager in District F. He told me that you applied for a store in his area. I told him he had to be mistaken since I told you I am not allowing you to move forward with the company right now regardless of what the rankings say. I cancelled your interview with him. You still owe me more time, and the area cannot afford to lose you right now." Tears of frustration ran down my face onto my phone. I typed several drafts but could not hit send.

For the rest of the weekend I pretended to be sick. I laid in bed the entire weekend to pretend like I had the flu, but I really had a broken heart. I did not look forward to the next minute because my pain was intensifying by the second. Sunday night snuck up on me quick. Monday was a day that I did not want to face. Even though Monday followed a tragic event, it was similar to everyday for the past few years. I was not looking forward to it. It is impossible to appreciate each day when you are not excited about being a part of it. If you don't enjoy your days it will turn into a life not enjoyed.

Chapter 17

Even though I woke up before sunrise almost every day I would sleep until the afternoon if my alarm clock did not go off because I was so burned out. That morning was different. I woke up Monday morning at 4:30am before my alarm could go off. I went outside and sat on my balcony to embrace this weird happening. I sat down for an hour and a half in a daze with no entertainment. God had to guide me to work because I didn't remember anything that happened on that commute. The windshield wipers could have been turned all the way up while it wasn't raining and I would not have recognized it. I stayed in a daze until Lucas showed up at work like nothing happened that past Friday. Right after Lucas came in, so did some special visitors. Head of ethics and loss prevention came from the corporate office to "randomly" do an audit of the branch. The morning was fast paced so there was not much interaction with them. Whenever things got busy at the branch we had a system in place. Ralph would wash cars while I handled the front with sales and Lucas would handle commuting customers to and from the branch. Things went smoothly for the first hour of work until Ralph and Nate tried to cross through the same door at the same time.

Nate took out the toothpick that he always had in his mouth then said, "Watch where you going you punk ass bitch." Ralph stared Nate down then said "I got your punk ass bitch right here". He then walked to the middle of the floor and said, "Fight me bitch! Right now!" Loss prevention broke it up and prevented the shop manager from taking an ass whipping. Shortly after breaking up the altercation and coming to the conclusion that everything was being ethically ran on my end they left. My work was already not respected as it should have been because people in the company did not know what I worked though on a daily basis and now it was given the perception that everything was out of control. My porter was doing credit card scams and my manager trainee was about to fight our most important vender. What perfect timing. Higher up visitors at companies make brief appearances at the local offices every so often. Whatever impressions that is set the day of their visit will remain in their head after they leave.

Nate immediately left the branch after the argument and we had no reservations until 12:00pm so I decided to take an early lunch. When I got to the restaurant where I was taking lunch at my legs became weak and I became lightheaded. As soon as I sat down Ralph called my cell phone and said, "Paul called the store phone several times in a row looking for you. I told him you were at lunch. He also asked did I know anything about you looking for jobs outside of the company. I told him no. He said he wants you to come to the corporate office at 3:00pm."

I was excited about the meeting with Paul. Maybe he came to his senses, and wanted to talk to me about moving forward with the company. Since I was getting off early I told Derrick to meet me with the person he wanted to link me with at a restaurant near the corporate office. Usually the drive to the corporate office was a forty-five minute drive from my branch but I took the street route instead of the interstate. I arrived to my destination at 2:45pm. Usually when I arrived there someone would rush to open the door for me when I rang the bell in the lobby. Paul symbolled for me to wait in the lobby when he saw me waiting by the lobby door. This was my first time I was asked to wait in the lobby since my third interview with the company. I sent Derrick a text as I saw Paul approaching the door.

Paul walked off as soon as he opened the door without greeting me. Not a word was spoken as we walked down the halls. Everyone who was in their offices and cubicles looked downwards as I walked past them. Even people who I

159

considered friends looked the other way. When we got to the back office which was occupied by the Human Resources manager, Paul asked me to wait by the door for a few seconds as he walked in the office. As soon as I sat down in the office Paul hunched over, then looked at my shoes and said, "You have been struggling to keep your customer service scores above corporate average and I have done all I can to help you. Also you have not been protecting company assets to our minimum expectations. You are the reason why Lucas did what he did. I hate to tell you this, but this is where we part ways. You are officially terminated."

A deer in headlights looked less caught off guard than me. It was as if someone unexpectedly pulled a gun out on me and it was too late. Before they opened their mouth I knew exactly what was about to take place. I just did not want to admit it to myself. When I sat down I had my rebuttal prepared because I knew my death with corporate America was in process but I saved it because I wanted to move on with my life as fast as possible. Paul and the human resources manager responded very similar to Todd and Roger after they fired me. They expected me to react violently and to act ignorantly out of my character. Regardless of me having a clean slate of never acting violent towards anyone and never verbally getting out of character I was stereotyped in a manner that most would deem racially motivated. "Thank you for the opportunity." I responded, and walked out the office. Paul followed me to the door. When I turned over the keys to my company car he asked, "Is there anything I could do for you?" I looked at him and said, "No, what I needed you to do, you didn't do."

Getting fired by Paul was the most vulnerable I felt in my entire life. By the time I realized what was going on it was too late to protect myself. Many people do not feel they are at war if someone does not make violent physical advances towards them or word gets out that someone is talking negatively about them. The war in Corporate America is fought more viciously than in the streets. The most dangerous opponents don't make it known they are at war. Gangsters in Corporate America smile with you, drink with you at happy hour, ask to see pictures of your family and pretend they care for you. But at the drop of a dime they would still be poised to destroy you if the opportunity presented itself. On the street, most gangsters carry weapons because they know the odds are higher that they will have to defend themselves. Not enough people in corporate America protect themselves properly. Even as a child and adolescent I learned how to maneuver different in life to protect myself from lessons that I learned growing up in the hood. Knowing I was at war with my ex-girlfriend and Caron spared my life. I bought Shooter along with me because I knew there was a chance that someone would try to slay me. He killed the person who tried to take my life. I called Hassan to pick me up outside of my ex-girlfriend's house because my instincts warned me that someone would be trying to kill me that night. The reason I texted Derrick as soon as I was asked to wait in the lobby was because I realized Paul was about to fire me and take my company car. I did not realize I was at war with Paul before it was too late. That's why I was a casualty of war with Todd and Roger also. My guards were down, and my enemies were attacking me while I was not even aware of it.

Derrick was waiting outside for me in the parking lot of the corporate office after I got fired. He got out of his truck and embraced me with a sympathetic handshake and hug. "I have someone in the backseat that you might remember." Derrick said with a grin on his face. The homeless man who I gave the bag of drugs to was sitting on the backseat with the most excited look on his face. He looked like an entirely different man. The only reason I remembered him was because he still had three teeth in his mouth and his voice was unforgettable. "I never looked back since you gave me that bag of drugs. I am rich now. I have to repay you. This bag of money is for you." he said. I refused the bag of money. God and the universe had spoken to me enough. I was given a plethora of signs to leave the streets of the hood and the streets of corporate America. He spared my life in the streets of the hood, but did not spare my life in Corporate America. The scars that can't be seen on the flesh hurts worse than ones that can. The one time in life that I made a dishonorable act I righted my wrongs and it came back around to bless me. God showed me I was able to adjust and flourish in any situation. It was obvious that my growth was limited working in Corporate America. The ceiling that was once placed over my head in corporate America transformed into a sky once I decided to become an entrepreneur. All of my life I have been continuously shown that God is invested in me. I did not want to take money from someone else, or use a loan to begin my business. God's investment in me was enough.

My main goal in life growing up was to make it out of the hood. That target was way too low. Everyone in the hood knows they should try to make it out. Most people who are employed in corporate America do not realize they should try to make it out until they have spent a considerable amount of time as an employee. As many dreams die in the hood as in corporate America. Making it out of corporate America should have been the main goal. I accomplished that along with my initial goal. Being outside of the hood doesn't mean you are free in this country. No employee is a free person, until they employ themselves. One day our story in life will come to an end when it is time to leave this earth. The worst way to live your life is to not know you were the author of your own story. The main motives in my life are to leave my knowledge and experiences in the universe to live on well after my physical death and to make my son proud. After coming home to my son after work days during my last job in corporate America I realized something. My son would be more proud of me if I was able to create a business and start a legacy instead of me being a top performer at a company that he would have to start from at the bottom. He would also be extremely proud of me if you read this.

Made in the USA
San Bernardino, CA
27 November 2018